# A DEAD QUESTION

Detective Inspector Honey Laird is two weeks away from giving birth when her boss asks her to investigate Dr McGordon ... her neighbour. On the outside he appears to be the perfect doctor, but when officers knock on his door, looking for witnesses to an accident, Dr McGordon reveals a guilty conscience about something and refuses to say anything. Honey, helped by an unsure young officer, her overprotective house-keeper and her faithful Labrador, Pippa, dives into the case, and it soon becomes clear that the 'what' can be just as mysterious as the 'who' ... and ultimately just as shocking.

# A DEAD QUESTION

# A DEAD QUESTION

*by*

Gerald Hammond

**Magna Large Print Books**
Long Preston, North Yorkshire,
BD23 4ND, England.

British Library Cataloguing in Publication Data.

Hammond, Gerald,
    A dead question.

    A catalogue record of this book is
    available from the British Library

    ISBN   978-0-7505-2751-4

First published in Great Britain 2007 by Allison & Busby Ltd.

Published in Large Print 2007 by arrangement with
Allison & Busby Ltd.

Magna Large Print is an imprint of Library Magna Books Ltd.

Printed and bound in Great Britain by
T.J. (International) Ltd., Cornwall, PL28 8RW

2923993

# Chapter One

Detective Inspector Honoria Laird, née Potterton-Phipps and therefore inevitably AKA Honeypot but universally known and referred to by friends and colleagues as Honey, was seated in the study of the Edinburgh home that she shared with Detective Chief Inspector Alexander ('Sandy') Laird, her husband and the soon-to-be father of her child. It was not in her nature to play second fiddle, even to a much-loved husband who had the advantage of being slightly the older and more senior of the two. She had therefore been using the leave, to which her pregnancy entitled her, to study the morass of papers in front of her. She was due to give evidence in several associated cases, one of them a murder, which were expected to reach the High Court soon and neither the date of the expected event nor those of the trials were within her control. It seemed to be the assumption of her superiors that, if she could produce the explanation of a death and three disappearances with all the finesse of a conjurer producing a rabbit, she could somehow manage to produce a baby without interrupting the flow of her evidence. Honey's motto might well have been No Challenge Too Great, but on this occasion she would have to trust to luck.

Honey was blessed with an excellent memory. Some would say that she had total recall. Nevertheless, studying comes hard when one is entering one's fourth decade. For a period only just ended, her pregnancy had seemed to be at risk and she had spent more than a little time in bed. She was bored and she felt in need of exercise.

She was tempted to seek relief in gardening but, quite apart from there being a bitter January wind, Sandy and several other people had absolutely forbidden her to do any physical work. This would not have been an end to the matter except that Sandy, who was more often the gardener, would certainly notice any signs of digging or pruning. Moreover, bending down was becoming increasingly difficult and straightening up again almost impossible. There was always the greenhouse, of course, where a whole range of cuttings were in need of repotting; that would hardly count as physical work, nor was the interior of the greenhouse strictly speaking 'out of doors', but Sandy might not take that enlightened view. She was rather hoping that some visitor would arrive and furnish an excuse to push aside her notebooks.

There seemed to be some chance of her wish being granted when the black Labrador at her feet, who had been deep in snoring and ~~farting~~ mode, awoke instantaneously and sat up. Somebody known to and approved by the bitch was about to arrive. Pippa was far from alone in this remarkable talent. How a dog can sense the imminent arrival of a visitor long before, by human standards, it could possibly have heard footsteps or recognised a vehicle, is a mystery still unsolved; but sure enough, some seconds later came the sound of a vehicle turning out of the street outside.

The Laird residence was a neat, Edinburgh house of the early nineteen hundreds, built by the hundred to a budget but at a time when space and quality were affordable and becoming ever more desirable. It was almost identical to its neighbours. It was, in fact, rather too large for a childless couple with one resident housekeeper, but it had been purchased with a view to the family which was now showing signs of arrival. It was even more desirable because it backed onto farmland and was not a terrace house like its neighbours but, being the last of the terrace, was semi-detached. The fact that Honey was the favourite child of a father who was an industrial tycoon and a major landowner had facilitated the purchase, but if Sandy was aware of the fact he tried to ignore it. Honey had become adept at making hidden contributions towards family extravagances. Sandy had poulticed his puritan streak and slightly leftish views by devoting most of his leisure time to decorating and modernising the house.

This end-terrace feature had enabled the original builder to squeeze in a small extra room against the gable of the house at ground floor level. This had probably been intended as a breakfast room, but it had drifted into use as a casual study and mini-library. A serving hatch left over from its previous function was convenient for the passing of occasional cups of coffee. Honey had chosen and Sandy had hung a restful paper of blue-grey with a faint bird pattern, but the walls had soon become largely hidden and the barely adequate floor space further reduced by book shelving crammed with a mixture of serious textbooks on law, forensics and policing together with a great many works of fiction or not too heavy non-fiction, all crammed in without the least attempt at methodical arrangement. The work of arranging the books methodically had been deferred, probably for ever, because of the inability of the two partners to agree any logical system that could also cater for varying sizes of books and spacing of shelves.

The remaining floor space was largely occupied by the desk at which Honey was sitting. This had been purchased cheaply when Police HQ had been re-equipped and would be replaced by something a little more sleek and efficient the next time that Honey could find a way to camouflage any such extravagance or to lose a substantial part of the cost among the bills for improvements to the heating and plumbing. The executive chair in which she was sitting had been a present from her father. That, at least, was her story.

The advantages of the round-the-corner placing of the room included a view of the sunlit garden of the larger house next door and also a reduction of the traffic noise from the busy street. The street, when new, had provided front gardens enclosed by neat and prim iron railings but these had been removed for scrap metal during World War Two. The Lairds' own front garden, like many others, had been largely sacrificed to interlocking brick parking space, only a line of azalea bushes being retained for cosmetic purposes. The disadvantage of this arrangement was that Honey could not see the visitor at her door and thus could not pretend to be absent if the visitor was unwelcome. (CCTV also figured in her list of future extravagances.) However, Pippa the Labrador had a taste in visitors that could almost always be trusted, with a very few exceptions.

This proved to be one of the exceptions. Honey was about to heave herself out of her chair – because there could be no doubt that the burden she was carrying was gaining weight – when she heard June's footsteps pattering past. June was the housekeeper. Her mother served Honey's father and family in the same capacity. June had set herself the impossible task of relieving Honey of any need to move again, at least for as long as the pregnancy lasted. On her return, she brought with her one of Honey's least favourite people.

How Pippa had come to develop a fondness for Detective Superintendent

Blackhouse Honey was quite unable to comprehend. Labradors, in their woolly minded way, are usually almost logical in bestowing their affection. First comes the person who can be counted on to take them for long and interesting walks, preferably with a gun. A very close second indeed comes the bringer of food. Next, if not the same person, is the brusher and groomer. Somewhere close to the tail-end are those who speak kindly, administer pats, or give a scratch in exactly the right place.

But Detective Superintendent Blackhouse was none of these. From the first, he had conceived an intense dislike of Pippa and although he had come to recognise her talent (and not a little luck) in contributing to the solution of more than one case, he had advanced no further into rapport with her than to administer a cautious pat now and again. Honey could only believe that Pippa, having seen Mr Blackhouse at work and watched hardened officers quail, had concluded that he must be the leader of the pack. She fawned around his feet in a manner that Honey could only consider an act of infidelity.

Mr Blackhouse was a large man, running to fat. Years of desk work had ruined his posture so that he seemed to be slumping, as if made out of melting candle-grease. Unlike the thousands of men promoted away from what they do well, he had been promoted out of detection in the field, in which he did not excel and only luck and an ability to ride on the backs of his juniors had enabled him to survive, and into supervision and management where, being a competent administrator, he passed muster. From the first he had taken one of his famous dislikes to Honey, to such an extent that she had spent her first few days on his team investigating dog turds. Honey, however, had not only produced good results in several cases but had even encouraged Mr Blackhouse to take full credit. This was a certain way to his heart. Unfortunately, he had never found a way to hers although he was quite unaware of the dislike in which she held him. Thereafter, he had fostered her career and even, to her disgust, insisted on appointing himself godfather-elect to the unborn child. This, presumably, could be expected to bring visiting privileges, but Honey was quite unable to think of any way to avert the disaster.

After telling Honey not to get up, which she had had no intention of doing, he seated himself uninvited on the only other chair and embarked on a series of questions about the health of mother and foetus that Honey would have considered intrusive even coming from her doctor. There could be no doubt that he had been sent forth, as usual, with his shoes shining and his clothes spotless and well pressed; but the effect was spoiled by the fit of his grey flannel suit. Honey judged that he had put on more weight since being measured for the suit and that, when being measured, he had drawn himself up into a better posture that he was unable to maintain.

Satisfied at last on the subject of her health, he got down to business. 'There's something I'd like you to take on for me,' he said.

'I'm supposed to be on maternity leave,' she pointed out.

'True. Quite true,' he said while making a dismissive gesture. 'But you can do this without a lot of rushing about. In fact, I wouldn't be surprised if you could do it without getting out of your chair, because it concerns one of your neighbours. And if you do this for me, I can arrange that the time spent on it doesn't count against your maternity leave.'

That put a different complexion on it. Sandy and Honey were planning to get away together with their daughter as soon as she was born, to stay on Mr Potterton-Phipps's

Perthshire estate. (Scans had revealed no sign of a male member.) Sandy had spent some time on secondment to the USA and had back-leave due. An addition to Honey's maternity leave would be a definite boon. She supposed that she could trust Mr Blackhouse just this far. 'You'd better tell me about it,' she said.

'There's somebody else I'd like to bring in.'

'Perhaps we'd better go through to the sitting room,' Honey suggested. 'We don't have space for another chair in here.'

'He can stand.'

With that unnecessary demonstration of his lack of consideration for others, Mr Blackhouse got up. Honey had time to notice that his bump was still larger than hers. He was absent for less than a minute. When he returned he had with him a tall young man in a sports jacket and grey trousers. The newcomer had a friendly but not unintelligent face. His hair was short, black and curly. He looked familiar.

'This is PC Dodson. Dodson, this is Detective Inspector Laird.'

The penny dropped. 'You were here a couple of days ago in the evening, in uniform, looking for witnesses to an accident.'

'Yes, Ma'am.'

Mr Blackhouse was not noted for patience with his subordinates. 'Get on with it, man,' he said. 'Tell the inspector.'

The Constable was standing stiffly to attention. 'And relax,' Honey said. The Superintendent looked surprised.

'Yes Sir. Ma'am. I was on house-to-house, looking for witnesses to the old body – lady, I mean – being knocked down at the lights on Thursday. I called here before going on to next door.'

'Was June able to help you at all?' Honey asked.

'No, Ma'am. She'd passed the place, but not at the right time. I went on to the Doctor's house.' The Constable nodded to the larger house that stood proudly out of the smart garden next door. Even in mid-winter there was colour in the garden, the red of dogwood, the yellow of witch hazel and sundry colours from early bulbs. The grass was unmarked. Honey envied that grass. There were dogs next door but they were limited to a back garden that was out of her view. Honey loved dogs but gardens and dogs were, in her opinion, an unsatisfactory combination.

'Go on. That's Dr McGordon.'

'Aye. So I found.' Dodson paused to gather

17

his thoughts. He was well spoken, probably grammar rather than a fee-paying school. His build was good, his clothes were clean and tidy and his shoes were well polished. Honey decided that girls might not pounce on him but they would take a second and a third glance and then decide that he was worth several more. 'My partner, PC Trimble, had been along the other side of the street, but he finished first and he was just coming to join me, leaving the car outside Dr McGordon's gate. I rang the bell. Dr McGordon came to the door himself. He had a glass in his hand and I could smell whisky. He was not quite drunk and yet he was by no means sober, just on the drunk side of in-between. He looked from me to my partner and then at the car by the gate.

'His face fell and he lost his colour. "I should have known that you'd come for me one of these days," he said. "I suppose I'll get sent away for this."

'I hadn't the faintest idea what he was on about, but it's my experience that if you can keep somebody talking, sooner or later he'll tell you all about himself. I couldn't think of any way to keep him talking on the doorstep without letting on that I was clueless, so I said something like, "Come down to the

18

station, please, and we'll sort it all out there."

'Without a word, he turned and put his glass down on the hall table and then he came out, locking the door carefully behind him. He got into the car like a lamb. I was going to hand him over to somebody more senior to deal with. But then Dave Trimble went and blew it, I don't know how. But he said, "Should we tell somebody, Sir? Your wife, perhaps?"

'Dr McGordon said, "Just a minute, what are you charging me with?" I said that we'd sort out the details of the charge at the station. He lost his haggard look and his expression began to change. It's not an easy face to read, it seems to have some expressions frozen onto it, but I was sure that he showed relief, then amusement came and went very quickly and he ended up looking angry and sort of sneering, which is much more like his natural expression. He said, "You don't know, do you?" I tried to tell him that I was only obeying orders but he was having none of that. "I've done nothing wrong," he said, "and my wife's in Canada. You can tell my housekeeper, if you like." We brought him in anyway, but by that time he was shouting for his solicitor and we soon had to let him go.'

## Chapter Two

Dr McGordon's garden remained peaceful beyond the window, as neat and respectable as an illustration in a gardening magazine. It was visited regularly by professional gardeners from a landscaping company and was always smart if lacking in imagination. It was a familiar scene to Honey, so familiar that it only registered when she sought solace in the tranquillity of it. It had in a way become that picture, stereotypically immaculate, so that the idea of crime, which she had seen in every other variety of scenery, was barely imaginable. They could hear, faintly beyond the double glazing, the midday traffic beginning in the street.

'I can see the difficulty,' Honey said. 'Any charge worded along the lines of *we know he's done something but we don't know what* cuts right across the basic principles of justice, because it opens the door to just plain locking somebody up. A competent solicitor would get it thrown out without ever coming to court.' She looked at PC Dodson. 'So, unless the good – or possibly not so good – doctor was pulling your leg, we know that he did something but we don't know what. Not a whodunnit, in fact, but a whadiddydo. Right?' Dodson nodded. Honey switched her gaze to the Detective Superintendent. 'But why give it to me? It needs a team keeping observation and asking ten thousand questions. It needs a collator with a computer looking for contradictions. It needs power to open up confidential records. It needs court orders. If ever there was a case needing facilities and resources, this is it.'

Mr Blackhouse had never been one to accept having his decisions questioned; but in this instance, although he looked thunderous, his thunderbolts were not directed at Honey. 'What it needs and what it gets may only fit where they touch,' Mr Blackhouse said grimly. He drew his left ankle up onto his right knee in an attitude that he probably thought of as macho but which exposed to view the cuff of his long johns and an unlovely sock suspender. 'We have nothing to go on except a few words uttered, with a drink in his hand, by a very reputable professional man. A professional man, I might add, who happens to number among his private patients a senior QC, a

21

sheriff, several councillors, two members of the Scottish Parliament, various relatives of very senior police officers and the Chairman of the Police Complaints Committee.'

'You checked, did you?' Honey asked.

'I was told in no uncertain terms to leave it alone. The order came from the Assistant Chief Constable (Crime) and was conveyed by his depute. Of course I checked. My sister-in-law attends the group practice. Can you imagine the scream that would go up if we were found to be harassing such a man on no stronger grounds than a few words uttered when he'd taken a drink? And against orders? Yet Constable Dodson here is sure that the Doctor is guilty of something and I'm sure he's right. I can feel it in my water.'

Honey refused to contemplate anything to do with Detective Superintendent Blackhouse's water. 'But why me?' she asked.

'I've checked up on young Dodson here,' said Mr Blackhouse. 'I'm told that he can keep his trap shut and I know that you can do the same. If I start to set up an inquiry into the Doctor, how long would it be before word got back to him, his friends and my bosses? On the other hand, you're away from the office. You're intelligent–'

'Thank you, Sir,' Honey said, 'I shall

treasure that remark.'

Mr Blackhouse's face fell into its customary expression of intolerant peevishness. 'Don't interrupt. And don't you be flippant, my girl. I was going on to say that you live next door to the man, so you must be able to see his comings and goings. And you must know a lot of people who know him. You have a dog that can sniff out drugs or a dead body in the most surprising places. I can borrow Dodson from Traffic and let you have him for a month or two to do your running around – we can give it out that he's teaching kids how to cross the road or something. You have a computer. Any facility that you want, ask me and I'll see if I can manage it without cooking up a storm, though I'm not too optimistic about that. I'm not expecting you to make a case against him,' the Detective Superintendent said generously. 'Just give me an honest and reasoned opinion as to whether there's anything to be dug up. I'll take it from there. Do we have an understanding?'

'I suppose so,' Honey said.

'Good, good. Keep me posted, word of mouth only. Don't get up. Dodson can see me out.' The Detective Superintendent rose with an effort to his feet and stood looking down at Honey. He seemed about to say more to her but in the end he just nodded and turned away. 'I'll take the car, Dodson. You can come back by bus when the inspector's finished with you.' The room looked a little bigger after he had left it.

When Dodson returned from speeding the Superintendent on his way, he was looking dazed. 'Come back in,' Honey said, 'and sit down.' She thought that the Constable looked rather young. This, she had heard, was usually to be taken as a sign that she was getting old, but perhaps he really was young. 'How long have you been on the Force?' she asked.

'Just under two years, Ma'am. Er, what do I call you?'

'Ma'am will do. Or Mrs Laird. Or Inspector. Guv'nor, if you like. When I get to know you better, we'll see.' Honey began to pack up her books. 'I do not usually encourage grumbling among those younger than and junior to myself, but if you wish to point out that we have been landed with an impossible task and nothing whatever to undertake it with, I shall not object.'

Dodson thought for a few seconds and then grinned suddenly. 'I would only be repeating what you just said, Ma'am.'

'True. You may not know it, but you have just passed your first test. In a minute I'm going to go into the sitting room and put my feet up. Doctor's orders, but I shall also occupy the time with a little thinking. I'll organise some lunch shortly. Meantime, you can use my computer – you can use a computer?'

'Yes, Ma'am.'

'Use it to write out a statement, as you told it just now but including every last detail that you can think of. We'll build our files in this computer and keep nothing on paper for the moment. First, let's think. You say the Doctor had been drinking but was in control of himself?'

'Yes, Ma'am.'

'But the drink had had some effect on him?'

'Yes, Ma'am.'

'What effect?' Dodson looked blank. 'Drink takes people different ways. Was he happy? Sleepy? Aggressive? Giggly? Lachrymose? That means tearful,' she added.

Dodson looked insulted. 'I do know what lachrymose means, Ma'am. It comes from the Latin for tears. But I don't think that he was any of those. His colour was up but he was quite steady on his feet. I've never heard

25

his voice at any other time but he didn't sound as if he was having any difficulty with his words. He just looked like a man who'd lowered his guard because he was relaxing with a dram.'

Honey looked at him for a few seconds but he accepted her regard passively, without fidgeting. 'You didn't have much to go on. The man came to the door with a glass in his hand and said a few words. You only had a few seconds of his body language and his tone of voice to go by.'

'I heard him say plenty in the car and in the station.'

'But by then his mood would have changed and so would your perception of him. You're sure that his first mood was not a joking one?'

'Ah!' Dodson caught up. 'You mean, was he in the sort of mood that when he opened the door and saw two coppers there his impulse was to say, "They've come to take me away, ha-ha," meaning it as a joke. That's what you mean?'

Honey tried not to lose patience. She reminded herself that Dodson had newly come from Traffic. He was a Woodentop. 'That's just what I mean. Think about it. If you'd stopped him when he was driving and he said, "It's a fair cop" in that tone of voice, would you have thought that he was joking? Or that he was in fear of the breathalyser? Think carefully. It's important.'

'I can see that, Ma'am.' Dodson thought about it. 'No, Inspector. Definitely not joking. He was surprised and for a moment he was horrified. He spoke without thinking, but it wasn't a joke.'

'And he hinted at prison? That suggests something serious. Any first offence short of GBH only nets you probation and community service these days, provided that you make enough of a show of contrition. But we shouldn't lean too heavily on that,' Honey said. 'He may have known that he was exaggerating. Or it may have to do with something that's no longer illegal – I don't suppose that he keeps pace with changes in the law. Now think. It was when your partner referred to the Doctor's wife that he suddenly realised that you didn't know what he had been talking about?'

'I think so, yes.'

'That needn't be significant. But Doctor McGordon's wife left him a year ago. She is or was a stout blonde woman – I use the past tense not because I think she's dead, although it's a possibility that we shouldn't forget, but because she may have managed to take some weight off. I never knew the Mc-Gordons but I suddenly stopped seeing her around and the word among the neighbours was that she had walked out after a disagreement and gone to her sister in Canada.'

Dodson registered enlightenment. 'Oh my God! If he'd killed her, that would explain his fear; and his relief when my partner asked if we should tell his wife. It told him how little we knew.'

'That's so,' Honey said. 'But don't get too hung up on that idea. There are other explanations.'

Honey had the nap on which those who watched over her – her nannies, she often called them when she was out of patience with being mothered – were wont to insist. It had been her custom to take a light lunch, little more than a snack in a crusty roll, but in view of her condition June insisted on serving a proper meal of a thin soup, cold meat with three vegetables and a syrup tart. Dodson, who ate with her, could hardly be fobbed off with less and seemed to feel that he had struck lucky. The meat was venison, the healthiest of meats; Honey's father had sent them a haunch. Dodson little knew that Honey's real fancy would have been for a pickled herring with peanut butter and a pomegranate, but she knew that any such eccentric desire would have triggered endless argument, followed by searches for those and other exotic and out-of-season foods.

Over lunch Honey studied, approved and later shredded a printout of Dodson's report. 'It's quite possible,' she said, 'that whatever the Doctor has on his conscience is something quite unrelated to his profession; a hit-and-run, perhaps. In fact, that's quite a possibility and we'd better keep it in mind. One can't visualise a doctor driving a getaway car. A deliberate venture into crime would seem out of character, but a hit-and-run would be quite on the cards. But I think our only possible *modus operandi* will be to consider what temptations surround a practising medic and we'll try to eliminate them one by one. Unless you have any better ideas?'

Dodson looked blank. Apparently the idea that he might be expected to think and even to come up with original thoughts was a new one to him and not one that was encouraged in Traffic. 'No Ma'am. Except perhaps to trawl through unsolved crimes, looking for one that might fit. There's murder of his patients for gain, Shipman-style.'

'And maybe practising euthanasia.'

Dodson had initially been terrified of Honey. She was not only his senior but she was also a woman; and not only that but she was beautiful, high ranking and blessed with the special glow by being pregnant. These factors added up to an intimidating figure. The discovery that she was both considerate and possessed of a sense of humour had gone a long way towards relaxing him. 'Drugs,' he added. 'And abortions.'

'I doubt if abortions are a very profitable sideline, in the present state of the law, but we'll keep them in mind. And bearing false witness in a claim for compensation against an employer or an insurance company.'

'Carrying on with female patients,' Dodson said.

'That's very good. Make a list and leave it on the computer and we can both add to it as we think of things.'

'Yes, Ma'am.' There was a silence as each tried to imagine other temptations to which a doctor might be exposed. Dodson broke it. 'After that, is there anything else that I could be getting on with?' he asked.

Honey stopped thinking about doctors' temptations and gave way to one of her own. Pippa, the Labrador, needed walking. June was just starting her half-day and would be going out to meet her boyfriend. Honey, now that she was carrying an extra person around with her, was much less enamoured of walking than usual. Her gynaecologist, who had at first urged her to carry on as normal, had then ordered her to bed during the period in which her foetus was believed to be in danger and had at last allowed her to resume real life but taking it easy, with plenty of rest and no periods of stress.

'You'll be visiting here quite a lot over the coming period,' she said. 'We don't want people to start thinking I've taken a lover.' (Dodson blushed and looked away.) 'You could be the dog-walker while I'm still carrying this bump around. If you go past Doctor McGordon's house, there's a lane goes into the farmland. You could walk up past the back of his garden. Let Pippa sniff around a bit. She has a talent for finding dead bodies, although the only candidate for that particular category disappeared many moons ago. You can do that?'

Dodson jumped to his feet. 'Of course, Mrs Laird.'

'Her lead's hanging in the hall.'

June was in a hurry to clear the dining room and get away. Honey paused in the study to add 'Baby-trafficking' to the list of temptations and then settled in the sitting room with her feet up, thinking. She dozed for a few minutes. When she snapped awake, the next step was clear in her mind. She only had to reach out her hand to pick up the cordless telephone extension. She keyed in the number from memory and held the phone several inches from her ear.

The phone was answered immediately with a reiteration of that number in a high and penetrating female voice. Honey flinched but persevered. Kate Ingliston was the most garrulous woman for miles around and with the loudest voice, but she lived opposite to Dr McGordon and she always knew all about everybody. On the other hand she had a heart of gold, Honey kept telling herself.

Honey submitted to the beginnings of an inquisition about the progress of her pregnancy. (Was there no woman, she wondered, who could accept the fact of her condition without wanting a kick by kick account of it? And no man who wouldn't make a bolt for the fresh air when offered any such insight?) When she managed to seize on a break in the flow, she said, 'But why don't you come over for a cup of tea? It seems ages since we had a good gossip.'

'I'll be over just as soon as I've finished this letter to Gwen in Cleveland because I must get it away today so that it'll reach her before she goes on holiday.' This was the shortest sentence that Honey could remember hearing her utter. 'She's going on a cruise to Mexico and through the Panama Canal and she wanted to know about what tours to take and so on, because you'll remember that Phil and I did that cruise a few years ago and some of the side-trips are marvellous but some are the absolute pits and you can get stuck at a mosquito-infested roadside for hours waiting for a coach because the train has derailed or something.'

'I'll go and put the kettle on,' Honey said. On her way to the kitchen she detoured into the study and added 'Malpractice' to the list that Dodson had begun. She was not quite sure what malpractice might comprise. She rather thought that it might be one of those omnibus words designed to encapsulate anything otherwise missed. She would look it up later.

What else might a doctor be tempted – or bribed – to do? She thought that Munchausen By Proxy Syndrome was a predominately female aberration. But serial killing? Bodkin Adams and Harold Shipman sprang to mind – and wasn't there some reason to believe that Jack the Ripper had been a doctor? – but there could be many, many more lurking unrecognised and unsuspected in the dark corridors of murder, simply because the odds are stacked in favour of a murderous physician, who has the knowledge, the means and the privilege of writing death certificates. It came to her that doctors were often required to give evidence in cases of accident or injury. A few seconds of consideration satisfied her that this could be a fertile field. She put 'Bearing false witness' on the list.

## Chapter Three

Honey had expected that anyone as verbose in speech as Kate Ingliston would require more than average time to write a letter, but it seemed either that her letter must already have been near completion or else that the lure of a good gossip outweighed the 'scribbler's itch'. Honey placed her tape recorder on the shelf below the coffee table and she had hardly carried a tray laden with the best china, the teapot, sugar, milk and a plate of sweet biscuits before the lady was at the door. Honey glanced quickly around. The sitting room, which was decorated in muted tones, the strong colours being imported with the furniture and pictures, looked immaculate. She had no wish to come second best in the house keeping stakes. She switched on the tape and went to admit her guest.

Kate was thin with brown hair that arranged itself in tight curls. Any pretence at beauty that she might have had was spoiled by an oversized nose. A sensible person so burdened would have made a joke of it but Kate was sensitive on the subject of noses. She had developed a knack of arranging herself so that the apparent size of her nose was at a minimum and the subject was best avoided altogether whenever she was present. Unfortunately, as Honey had discovered, there were many synonyms for nose and they seemed to leap forward, pleading to be used, whenever Kate was present. Kate's everyday clothes came from the medium price range but were so hastily chosen in colour, cut and style that Honey longed for an excuse to take her in hand. Honey was always saddened that such a good accent should be allied to such a strident voice.

During the week, Kate was a makeover waiting to happen.

On most weekends, the caterpillar became a butterfly as she and her husband sent the two children to stay with an unsuspecting grandmother and left for one of the more luxurious country hotels. Among their friends, they made no secret of the fact that they would be joined by one or more other couples for a weekend of golf and sex. For those occasions, Kate would be made up with great care and dressed in the latest and best; general opinion was that she put herself in the hands of an image specialist to choose her party wear and design her make-up. Honey could only suppose that, on those occasions, Kate had the sense to speak little if at all. It was hard to imagine the most dedicated lover remaining inflamed with passion while being battered by that voice.

As soon as they were settled in the sitting room, Kate returned to her queries about the state of health of Honey and her foetus, interspersing the replies with stories from one or other of her own pregnancies. Honey had been enjoying the process and looking forward to the moment of birth, but she was beginning to regret ever having set foot on that road. She was, however, soon offered the chance to turn the conversation in the direction that she wanted it to take.

'To tell you the truth,' she said, not quite truthfully, 'I get very bored. Of course, your house has a better outlook than mine does. This room only looks across the street to a house that's empty all day. You look over Dr McGordon's garden and past it to all the hills.'

'It's a nice view,' Kate agreed, 'and I can look at it for long enough, especially in the morning when I'm looking at the sunlit side of things. There's always something happening even if it's only a couple of rabbits having it off, which I must admit doesn't take them very long. But you must have the same view from the back of this house.'

'I only have the kitchen, the dining room, a bathroom and one bedroom facing that way. And you look over the Doctor's garden, which always seems to have something in flower. We only have one tiny room facing that way.'

Kate made a face dismissive of all species of flora. 'But flowers never seem to do anything very much, I mean I know that in fact they're copulating like mad at certain times of the year but never when I'm looking at them and anyway I can't see a

37

pair of hydrangeas having it off ever being much of a turn-on, can you?'

'Not a lot, no.' Honey gave up trying to lure the conversation to where she wanted it to go and adopted more direct tactics. Kate's conversation so often seemed to gravitate towards sex. 'You used to be pally with Mrs McGordon, didn't you. Wasn't she the gardener in that family?'

'She spent a lot of time in the garden. You probably used to see her from that little room you have that looks sideways, but she did more harm than good because, frankly, the green on her fingers was arsenic, I mean she couldn't tell a weed from an alpine and when she pruned a shrub you could count on her to take off all the shoots that would have flowered the next year. The azaleas are doing much better now and, honestly, I think she did the garden more good in her going than if she had stayed.'

Honey tried to hide a slight shiver. She hoped that Mrs McGordon was not doing her garden good by being buried in it. 'Tell me about her,' she suggested. 'Why did she leave? Do you know?'

Kate nodded and smiled. The light of the born gossip shone in her eyes. 'I probably know as much as anybody, which isn't a lot because I got a different story from each of them and I don't suppose anybody else got any more out of those stories than I did. I was in the Border Bookshop one day, looking for a present for Phil – I got him a book about antiquities, you know how he goes potty about archaeological digs and so on – and when I went upstairs for a coffee I saw the Doctor sitting all on his own, and most of the chairs were taken so of course I joined him.'

'Of course,' Honey said.

Even that momentary break had given Kate time to draw breath. 'I thought perhaps he was waiting for Dulcie so I asked after her and he seemed rather evasive so in the end I asked him point blank if anything was wrong, because she'd been looking a bit peaky and I wondered whether her diverticulitis had flared up again. And he drew himself up, very hoity-toity, not at all in his usual hail-fellow-well-met style that most people find so overpowering, and said that it depended what you meant by wrong and did I know that his wife had a lover, and if I did he'd be very much obliged if I told him who it was.'

'And who was it?' Honey asked before she could stop herself.

'I haven't the faintest idea,' Kate admitted reluctantly, 'but if it was true that she had a lover it was nobody I know, I'm quite sure of that, not unless it was another woman, because no man can ever resist dropping very subtle little hints, especially to a woman, the sort of hints that you have to be alert to see and read, all sort of saying, "Somebody finds me irresistible so you may as well join the club," you know what I mean?' (Honey knew exactly what she meant but she shook her head.) 'So I began to tick off all the people I could be sure it wasn't and he seemed to be getting more and more annoyed until in the end he gulped down what was left of his coffee and went down to look through the DVDs, which was probably a bluff because they didn't have a DVD player at that time although he bought one a few months later.

'I went straight home and I must have beaten him to it because his car wasn't there, but who should come knocking on my door a few minutes later but Dulcie McGordon, saying that she was leaving Duncan and wanting to know if I would store some of her things until she sent for them? I said that of course I would and was there anything else I could do, and she must really have been wanting a shoulder to cry on because she came in for a vodka and tonic and poured out her side of the story.

She swore blind that she didn't have a lover and never had but that nobody could have blamed her because Duncan had gone impotent for no physical reason and he wouldn't go to a therapist, not for anything, he was trying Viagra and it wasn't doing a bit of good and so he'd started blaming her which she said was horribly unfair because she'd tried everything the books and magazines suggested without the least effect, and I couldn't help agreeing with her – that it was unfair, I mean, because she told me some of the things she'd tried in order to give him a kick start and she didn't seem to have missed anything out – and she said that she was going to her sister in Canada.'

Honey framed her next question carefully. Kate was incapable of answering a question with a yes or no. 'From what you say, she must have given you her address in Canada. Do you still have it?' she asked. 'I have her on my Christmas card list because she sent me one last year. I've written the card but now I don't know where to send it.'

Kate was nodding cheerfully. 'I know I still have it because I was looking for another address this morning – my cousin Elsie, did you meet her when she was over here in the spring to settle her daughter in at Strathclyde University, doing engineering of all things? – and I came across it, so I'll let you have it.'

'I'll be very grateful. There's a son, isn't there?'

'Two sons, but Ian left home before you moved in here, he's working in accountancy down in the Borders somewhere but George is still nominally at home with his father, at least that's the address he uses for letters. He did Scots Law in Edinburgh and he's working for the Council, but I'm not surprised you don't know him because you hardly ever see him here, what with a very dishy girlfriend with a flat in the Old Town and playing a lot of golf, very successfully, plays off a two handicap I'm told, whatever that means.'

Honey had no intention of trying to explain a two handicap. 'Does he drive a green sports car?' She asked.

'That's right. You must have seen him some time that his girlfriend had gone off him.' Kate paused and looked at her watch and compared it with the carriage clock on Honey's mantel. 'Heavens above, is that the time? The children will have gone to their granny but Phil said he'd be home about now and he's carrying me off to some dinner thing in Glasgow in aid of lifeboats or Africa or something so I'll have to go and put my face on.'

Honey was suffering a surfeit of information that she wanted to digest before proceeding, and her ears were beginning to ring, but there was one more area that she wanted to explore. 'Before you go,' she said, 'tell me this. You said something about Dr McGordon's manner putting people off.'

Kate settled down again. This was too good a topic to neglect. 'Oh, it does, it does. He's usually the backslapping extrovert, or if he doesn't slap you on the back he'll shake your hand and crush it at the same time, and people can only take so much of excessive goodwill. Hasn't he slapped your back a time or two?'

'I've only passed him dog walking,' Honey said, 'and nodded to him from a distance. If he puts people off like that, how does he come to have such a distinguished list of private patients.'

'I don't know that of my own knowledge,' Kate admitted, 'I never needed a doctor except when I was pregnant and I wouldn't let that sort of hearty man get as close to me as that. But according to Phil he's a brilliant diagnostician, his reputation is that you can go to him with two separate but associated disorders and the symptoms confused by medication and he'll want to know every single symptom that you've had in the past year and he'll puzzle it out straight away and either prescribe the right medication or refer you to the right consultant, one way or the other he'll drag you through it and have you singing and dancing. And now I must fly. We'll do it again some time.'

'We certainly will,' Honey said.

She pushed herself upright and escorted her guest to the front door. Constable Dodson was just approaching, being dragged along by Pippa. Pippa was in her seventh heaven. She had been rolling or swimming in something absolutely appalling. The smell, Honey decided, was mostly of cattle dung along with well-rotted silage and just a hint of fox droppings. It made her eyes water.

Dodson was close to tears. 'I couldn't help it, Mrs Laird. She jerked the lead out of my hand and made off.'

'My fault,' Honey said. She waved to the amused but departing Kate, who would doubtless put the story all round the Central Belt by way of the evening's charity dinner. 'I should have warned you,' she told Dodson, 'that she loves a good roll and the smellier the better as far as she's concerned. Well, that settles it. Your next job is to take her round to the back of the house. The blessing of being the end house is that there is a path from front to back without taking a foul dog through the house and leaving a trail of perfume that will hang around for weeks. I'll pass you out the end of the shower spray and the shampoo. After that, you can come in and listen to the tape of the progress I've made.'

While Dodson showered and dried Pippa over the drain behind the house, Honey put her hand out to pick up the phone, but it rang before she could complete the move. Kate was on the line with the address of Dr McGordon's sister-in-law in Canada. Kate was unusually curt, but Honey could hear Phil, Kate's husband, making hurry-up noises in the background. 'I must just do this or I'll forget it,' Kate answered him – over her shoulder, to judge from the reduced volume. Honey thanked her quickly and rang off. While it was in her mind, she added 'Defrauding the NHS' to the list.

Dodson came in with Pippa. 'You are a damp scamp,' Honey told Pippa severely. 'A wet pet. A soggy doggy. Be ashamed, be very ashamed.' Pippa lay down and thumped her tail, still pleased with herself. Dodson was

45

now wetter than the dog but at least neither of them smelt too bad. Honey made sure that the dog towels were hung over the boiler. She gave Dodson a large carrier bag to open out and sit on. They listened to the tape together. Dodson proved modestly knowledgeable about computers and managed to transfer the contents of the tape to the computer before Honey set the recorder to tape some music and thus expunge the conversation.

'That lady doesn't half bend your ear,' Dodson said, 'but she'll be a useful source all the same.'

'There's a lot more to be got out of her,' Honey agreed. 'The pity is that I have to listen to ten minutes of irrelevance for ten seconds of gold dust. You'd better pop off home and get some dry clothes on. I'm going to phone Canada in the hope of tracking down Mrs McGordon. I'll keep a telephone record for you to listen to. Here's what I want you to make a start on tomorrow...'

DCI Sandy Laird parked his nearly new Vectra and gave his wife's car his usual baleful look. He was pleased with his own car and would have been proud of it. He polished it regularly and with a little encouragement might even have licked it clean. But Honey's father made a point of bestowing his Range Rovers on his daughter, recovering each for trading-in against the next. Because of representations from his senior managers and directors, who felt inhibited from indulging their more extravagant fancies in transport if the big boss was driving around in a humdrum tin box, Mr Potterton-Phipps only bought from the absolute top of the range. He then changed them, his son-in-law thought sourly, whenever the ashtrays were full of cigar butts. The contrast did not show his Vectra to best effect. Sandy had married for love and was horrified that anyone might think that he had married his wife because of her father's money. He was always careful to stand on his own feet, so to speak, but he did sometimes feel that he might bend his rule a little if Mr Potterton-Phipps would, just once, not reclaim Honey's car to trade in against an even newer acquisition but would allow her to pass it on to him. Honey would certainly have had no objection and her father would probably never have noticed, but pride prevented him from making the suggestion.

His wife was on the phone. He stooped to offer her a kiss but she turned her cheek instead of offering her lips, as she would previously have done without thinking about it. He tried not to show hurt and settled into his usual chair. Perhaps the days of wine and roses were over and he was going to have to take a back seat, play second fiddle, whatever the most apt metaphor might happen to be. Fathers, he had heard, were often relegated to the position of provider and occasional entertainer. Or nappy-changer. Well, if that was what the future held, so be it.

If a beautiful woman can be said to look furtive that is how Honey looked, but she proceeded with her call anyway. 'Is that really you, Rodge? Seems like I've been chasing you all over Montreal.' Her voice had adopted a trace of a transatlantic accent and discarded its usual unexceptionable grammar. She had a knack of matching her voice to the other's expectation. 'Yes, it's me, Honeypot, but they don't call me that any more, not if they want to live. I'm Mrs Laird now and a detective inspector, how does that grab you...? Yes, I thought it might. I'm looking for a favour. Do you have a pal in or around Vancouver? He'd be RCMP, I suppose... You do? Well I hope he's a good pal, because I want you to get him to help me out. I need to know if a Mrs Dulcie McGordon, divorced or separated wife of Dr Duncan McGordon, is still living with her sister, a Mrs Hopgood, at one-six-four-three Braintree Avenue. Treat it as urgent. And listen, Rodge, this is vital. Information to me, please, personally, I'll give you my number and email address in a minute, and he's not to make any waves. Not a single word to anyone but me. Yeah, it's one of those. The man I'm looking at has some big-wheel friends and there remains the possibility that he may not even have put a foot wrong...'

Sandy waited until the call had finished. 'Who is Rodge?' he asked.

'Just a Canadian I met on a security course, before I ever met you,' Honey said. Her tone was cool; Sandy could have put a little more effort into a proper kiss. Had pregnancy made her repugnant? She was careful not to sound defensive but she had known Rodge Hampton rather well. Since marrying Sandy Laird she had been as pure as the driven snow, but Sandy had a suspicion that her earlier life might have been rather less whiter than white. She was a remarkably attractive woman, her attractiveness enhanced by her seeming to be unaware of it, but in addition to being attractive she had, until pregnancy had brought about a change, been very appreciative of the joys of sex. In common with most men, Sandy preferred to know as little as possible about any earlier amours that his wife might have enjoyed and he still struggled to believe that she had arrived at the married state still unsullied.

'What's going on?' Sandy asked.

Honey chose to interpret his words as referring to the phone call. She had no secrets from Sandy. Well, very few. 'I'll tell you,' she said. 'You may even be able to help. What do you know about Dr Mc-Gordon next door?'

'Not a lot.'

'Come on, Sandy. You're a trained detective. What do you know?'

'Not to say know. He seems well heeled, but doctors in private practice don't exactly starve. He has a good reputation as a doctor. If you've got it, he'll find it and cure it. There's never been a whisper about him messing with his women patients. I met him at the golf club once; he was somebody's guest but his host had to leave him alone because of a suddenly urgent committee meeting and we had time for a chat.'

'What did you think of him?'

'I couldn't thole the bastard. Why?'

Honey began the story of her day. Sandy relaxed. At least a minor investigation conducted from home should keep her out of mischief for a while. Her threshold of boredom was very low; and when Honey was bored there was no saying where her craving for interest might lead her. He still recalled with nausea the occasion when a lull in her professional workload had led her to take up arms against a senior detective who, in her opinion, was not treating his wife with the consideration that, again in Honey's opinion, she deserved.

## Chapter Four

Honey awoke next morning in a mood of mixed indignation at being saddled by Detective Superintendent Blackhouse with a task that no reasonable person would have considered either possible or permissible; and a contrary relief at a break to the monotony of her gestation, even a distraction from the discomforts of bosom, belly and bladder. She struggled conscientiously through a set of gentle exercises designed to leave her in reasonable trim when the great event was past. To her surprise, she felt a stirring of a sensation that she thought was gone, perhaps forever – her old energy. Passivity had run its course.

Four brothers had preceded Honoria, so becoming a grandfather was not a new experience for Mr Potterton-Phipps. But Honey, as the only daughter, had a special place in his heart and he was stirred enough by the imminent addition to his dynasty (even if that branch of it would bear another name) to issue orders, whenever any member of his entourage was going in the direction of shops, for the purchase of suitable items of maternity wear and other gifts. In addition, her sisters-in-law were only too happy to clear space in their respective houses by passing on the gifts with which they had been inundated. Honey was thus in a position to furnish an orphanage with playthings, and determined to do so as soon as the new arrival's preferences were established. She was so well equipped with prams and pushchairs that the second spare bedroom was unusable. More to the immediate point, she had an ample selection of clothes to fit all occasions, all stages of pregnancy and all weathers. After breakfast, she had no difficulty in kitting herself out for a short walk; although she did spare a sigh for the beautiful clothes being left behind in her wardrobe to become outdated by changing fashions.

June was horrified when Honey made clear her intention. Her round face dropped and her always-unruly hair took on a new life. 'You ken fine the Doctor said you were to stay inside!'

'He said nothing of the sort, so don't you go putting words into his mouth. He only said I wasn't to get chilled,' Honey retorted.

'He said no exertion!'

'He said no undue exertion. But I'm over-due for a little exercise. If you and Sandy had your way,' Honey said hotly, 'you would turn me into a sort of queen termite, lying help-less in bed, being fed by slaves and produc-ing babies by the dozen.' She paused to consider what she was saying. But no. Even a life of constant sex must eventually pall. 'Well, I'm not going to put up with it. I'm well wrapped up and I'm going out for a very short walk with Pippa, not to climb Everest.'

'Pippa will pull. And suppose your waters break while you're out!'

'I'm not due yet. And if they do, I'll phone you.' Honey waved the mobile phone.

'You're getting very close. And your ankles will swell.'

It was a telling threat. Honey held her

peace but made up her mind not to go far and to put her feet up on her return.

'I'll tell Mr Laird.'

'You do that thing.' With honour satisfied, Honey left the house, only to realise that in her vexation she had forgotten Pippa. She made a humiliating return. She gave Pippa a shake by the scruff of the neck. 'If you pull, you go for cat-meat,' she promised. The threat was greeted with a wave of the tail but it sometimes had the desired effect.

Outside again with Pippa on the extending lead, she found that the day was less attractive than it had looked from the comfort of the house. The sunshine, which had looked warm and tempting, was thin and ephemeral and there was a chill to the stiff breeze that penetrated even a thick, tweed coat. Carrying the extra weight took a lot of the joy out of walking – it was, she thought, rather like carrying a heavy haversack on the front instead of the back – but they turned downhill past the front of the Doctor's house. Kate was at the window of her sitting room. Honey gave her a wave and Kate responded with an unintelligible signal in which drinking from a cup figured. Honey nodded violently but walked on. The Doctor's garden, seen from the road, held a viburnum in full flower and a fine display of berries on a variegated holly. What, she asked herself, was the good of a garden that showed flowers for only half the year, if that? Her baby was going to see flowers all year round. But there were flowers in plenty in neighbouring gardens. She would get on the Internet and find out what plants could be counted on to flower during the Scottish winter.

Beyond the Doctor's garden they turned into a narrow lane that ran between the garden wall and the gable of a block of shops and flats. They emerged into a rougher lane that ran along behind the houses. Honey turned again to pass the back wall of Dr McGordon's garden. She noticed for the first time that there was a gate in the wall but that a line of weeds grew thick below it and the bolt, latch and hinges were thick with rust. So if anything incriminating had been carried from the garden to the farmland it must have gone round by the road. But why would the Doctor bury a body in farmland behind his house when he had available one large garden as well as his car, the whole of Scotland and probably one or more medical incinerators?

She walked on slowly, slightly uphill, past her own back gate. It needed paint. She had been brought up in the country. It was good to walk in farmland again, even in midwinter when wildlife was at its scarcest. Pippa began to pull hard towards a midden but Honey stopped her, sat her and reminded her that pulling was the slowest way to get to any destination. Of course, she mused, the Doctor's conscience-stricken gaffe need not relate to murder; she had been involved in too many homicides and her mind was beginning to see murder when there was none. She ran her mind over the list of temptations now lingering as magnetic images in the computer. How to get that sort of information without whistling up a storm? Her father's industrial network had sources, of course...

She was suddenly back in the here and now. She wondered why. And then she saw a fellow dog-walker descending the track towards her with a pair of German short-haired pointers at heel. It was the Doctor. To turn back would only attract attention. She walked on, not making eye contact. Perhaps a neighbourly nod would be enough...

It wasn't. As they met, the Doctor slowed. He was a large man, made apparently larger by his high colour, red hair and tweed suit in very loud checks. His clothes had been expensive and she noticed that his boots were of top quality and were polished almost to a mirror finish. The hair on his head was neatly trimmed, he was well shaved, but his eyebrows were overgrown and curly red hairs escaping from his ears and nostrils glowed in the backlight of a stray sunbeam. 'Hullo,' he said. 'I think you're my next door neighbour. It seems strange that we've never met. You've had that house for what? Two years now?' His voice was loud, his accent educated.

'Almost that,' Honey admitted. 'It seems that our hours of coming and going never coincide. I'm Honoria Laird.'

'Duncan McGordon.' They shook hands. It would have been easy to read far too much into his grip. She tried to detect undercurrents passing from hand to hand but there was only the dry brush of skin. He was smiling sociably but she wondered whether his smile was quite sincere. 'You're married to a policeman, I believe.'

Honey decided that the statement was correct. She was indeed married to a policeman. It seemed unnecessary to mention that she too was of the police. Agreement would not be committing her to a lie that might rebound. She said, 'Yes.'

Pippa was becoming impatient. She gave a pull on the lead, wanting to socialise with the two pointers that were waiting correctly a few yards away. Honey saw the Doctor's eyes go down. Immediately, she felt defensive on Pippa's behalf. 'She's taken to rolling in the most horrible things she can find, so she spends a lot of time on the lead. She's very obedient and a very good retriever, but rolling is the one habit I can't break. And if there's one thing I loathe it's bathing a dog – especially while I'm in my present state.'

'I do understand.' He smiled again. Honey tried to categorise the smile. Was it the smile of the tiger, of a crocodile, of the Cheshire cat, or could it be the smile of a cuddly toy? No, not that. But it was only a slight shift of the facial muscles around the mouth and eyes, too fleeting to judge. Whether it was sincere and sympathetic she was left with no idea.

They talked about dogs for an innocuous minute. The Doctor was evidently a well-informed dog-lover. Honey, who usually found a shared love of the canine species to be a first step towards lasting friendship, began to wonder whether he could have done anything so very terrible after all; but then she recalled that many psychopaths were sentimentally attached to pets and family. She limited herself to a few words of wisdom gleaned from her own experience and from many hours spent with her father's game-keepers.

The breeze was getting up and she allowed the Doctor to see her shiver. He took the hint, looked at his watch and said that he was due to hold a surgery shortly. He added that now that they'd met they must stay in touch. He shook her hand again and walked on, leaving her wondering. Had his manner been in the least suggestive? When one person attempted to judge another's character from facial movements of less than a hair's breadth, it was her experience that they often got it wrong. Had the eye that he cast over her figure been salacious or merely a professional assessment of her pregnancy? Now that she had met him, what was she prepared to believe of him? She reminded herself that whether she liked or disliked the Doctor – and she had no immediate idea which was the case – was irrelevant. She had known and liked several criminals in the past and conceived a hearty dislike for a number of suspects who had later proved perfectly innocent at least of the crime in question. A person, after all, may be aggressive or patronising, a bully or a coward or even have smelly feet without contravening any laws.

She had no intention of becoming his patient – as Kate had suggested, his manner did not suggest a lack of libido. Did he make a habit of referring his women patients early to a gynaecologist? Perhaps he would accept Constable Dodson as a National Health patient. But there were two snags to that idea. One, Dodson was in perfect health and, two, he was male. Honey recalled seeing a not unattractive WPC around with one arm in a sling. Perhaps she should ask Mr Blackhouse for her secondment.

She realised suddenly that she had walked further than she had intended. The pleasure of being out and about had become a burden. She dragged Pippa away from a cowpat and turned for home.

Mr Potterton-Phipps was being at his most elusive. After an hour spent in trying to contact her father by phone, twice just missing him as he left one office for another, Honey decided to settle for an email. Her father, she knew, had everything available to ensure the security of his personal electronic mail. She wrote:

*Dad,*

*Many thanks for the last parcel but no more*

*please until further notice. I now have enough maternity wear to see me through my next hundred and twenty pregnancies and more toys than any reasonable child could play with by the time he or she can vote. I am properly grateful but enough is rather more than enough.*

*If however, you still want to do me favours, I could use a little help. I have been set the problem of finding out why an outwardly respectable doctor seems to have a guilty conscience about something unspecified. He is Dr Duncan McGordon, of Deansfoot House, my next door neighbour in fact. The problem is that nobody must know that he is being investigated. Your various commercial interests have sometimes managed to produce sensitive information in the past and without making waves. Can they do it again? I'd be most interested in his financial standing and creditworthiness and also any unusual transactions in which he is involved.*

*Foetus and I are doing well together but looking forward to the day when she will pop her head out into the air, blinking at the sudden flood of light. You will certainly be among the first twenty or thirty to be notified. Do you have any strong views about names? There is hardly a female name in the thesaurus that one or the other of us has not had an unfortunate clash with a bearer of it.*

With that dispatched, she felt free to spend some time surfing the Internet. She got a useful list of winter flowering garden plants and printed it out for the garden centre, but if there was any concise list of what doctors are forbidden by law to do, as opposed to naughtiness within the ambit of the General Medical Council, she failed to find it. Something along the lines of the Ten Commandments would have been useful. Criminal law covered all the temptations on her list.

She burrowed into the Telephone Directory, then called Directory Enquiries and after a struggle she tracked down the Audit Department of the National Health Service. She found herself speaking to a contralto voice that identified itself as Prue Bishop, Area Supervisor.

Honey, in turn, revealed her standing as a detective inspector. 'I'm just doing a statistical update,' she said. 'Do you have many ongoing cases of GPs suspected of overcharging the NHS?'

'Quite a few,' Ms Bishop replied. 'Do you want dentists as well as doctors?'

Honey made a face in the mirror. Such a gaffe might start Ms Bishop doubting her story. 'Just GPs for the moment,' she said.

'I'll get back to you on dentists when we get around to that statistical area.'

'That sounds harmless. I can get that information for you now. Hold on a moment while I look. Yes. We have one prosecution in hand and eight under investigation.'

'So many?'

'It sounds a lot, but most will probably prove perfectly innocent. It often turns out to be sloppy bookkeeping by office staff. When doctors take on staff, sometimes they engage somebody capable of keeping accounts but just as often they only want a receptionist or a typist. Sometimes they offer the job on the basis of the best figure or the most tempting smile and they only introduce the subject of the bookkeeping system as an afterthought.'

'Of course. Doctors are human too, although they prefer one to imagine them walking on water. Just for the record, could I have the names?'

A perturbed sound came down the wire. 'I couldn't possibly give out that sort of information over the phone, not without some sort of identification. Give me your extension number and I'll call you back.'

'That's very helpful of you,' Honey said, 'but there's a snag. I'm at a rather advanced state of pregnancy so I'm filling in time, working from home.'

Ms Bishop's voice became much more animated. 'Are you really? So am I. Seven months gone and counting. When are you due?'

'Within two weeks,' Honey said. 'She's turned over but the head isn't engaged yet.'

'Well, lucky you! I can hardly wait for it all to be over. I was thinking of going out to my cousin in South Africa. I had a vague idea that it was already September there, but my partner pointed out that it may be late summer there but that that doesn't change the body clock. After the baby's born, of course, the difficult part is still only beginning.'

'They tell me that the first thirty years are the worst,' Honey said agreeably.

Ms Bishop gave a trill of laughter. She was a cheery woman with a sense of humour to match Honey's. They spent several minutes discussing the joys of pregnancy. Honey rather hoped that the other's reservations were being forgotten, but when the subject of maternity was considered exhausted for the moment Ms Bishop said, 'Well, when will you be in the office again? I could call you there?'

Honey gave in to *force majeure*. 'I'll try to

get into the office tomorrow. I'll call you and you can call me back. Or even better, I may have my husband call you and save me the trip. He's an officer too. Will that do?'

'That will do very well. I'll give him a talking-to about letting his wife work so long into a pregnancy. Good luck!'

'While you're about it,' Honey said, 'you could bring up the subject of snoring.'

'Don't talk to me about snoring,' Prue Bishop said. 'Being kicked from the inside and deafened from the outside, I don't know when I last had a good night's sleep...'

The problem of sleep deprivation took up several more minutes before getting onto the subject of food fancies. They agreed to meet at some future date to share a curried rhubarb tart. 'But it's now that I want it,' Ms Bishop said sadly. 'In a year's time I may not fancy it at all.'

'I know exactly what you mean,' Honey replied. 'The only compensation for being stretched and overloaded and thoroughly upset is having enormous cravings and making everybody run around in circles to satisfy them; and feeling guilty but happy about it all.'

'And then saying that perhaps you don't fancy it after all,' said Ms Bishop.

## Chapter Five

Honey lunched alone. Sandy, even when not pursuing the interests of justice in the furthest-flung corners of Lothian and Borders, was usually too busy to get home for lunch. June's mother, who was Mr Potterton-Phipps's housekeeper, had drilled into her daughter a due respect for her employers, a respect that June was inclined to honour when it suited her. Thus June, though feeling free to argue the point whenever she disagreed with Honey (she stood too much in awe of Sandy ever to gainsay him), never joined them at table except when invited on special occasions such as Christmas or her own birthday. This enforced solitude, though unsettling for one of Honey's sociable disposition, did at least allow her to read while she ate. She carried her quiche and salad through into the study and looked again at the theories so far accumulated. She was unimpressed. There was no category of crime on the list which she could envisage Dr McGordon committing, but for lack of anything more credible she felt obliged to soldier on.

The obligatory postprandial rest over, Honey decided to walk again. She had been fitter even than most men before pregnancy struck. There had followed the period when her ability to hold on had been in doubt and she had been ordered to spend long periods abed. That threat now lifted, she was determined to get her legs working again. Despite the added weight, she had returned at last to a state wherein she felt both energetic and in need of exercise. June protested in vain. The day was cooler but the breeze had dropped and the sunshine was almost warm. She put a small apple in her pocket and set off.

Kate was at her window again, signalling with a mixture of a drinking mime and a beckoning motion for Honey to come in for tea or coffee. Honey signalled back with what she hoped would be taken for *later, I'll call in after my walk*. The Doctor's car, a handsome Daimler, was either away or safely locked in the three-car garage at the further gable. A round female figure with a white apron came out of a side door, took something down off a washing line partly concealed by a hedge and retreated again. They followed their previous route but Honey persisted and, puffing slightly, climbed higher up the slight hill to where she could look over half the city, catching a glimpse of the Firth of Forth and the coast of Fife beyond.

When they were well past the midden, she let Pippa off the lead. During Honey's long period of rest, Pippa had not had the exercise that a Labrador is entitled to expect. Sandy had been busy and June considered a hundred leisurely paces on grass to be as much exercise as any living being could possibly need. Pippa stretched out in a good gallop over the pasture while her mistress, who often thought best in the open air with a distant prospect in view, took a seat on the rim of a cattle-trough and mentally sorted through the lines of enquiry open to her. Her legs were slightly shaky from the unaccustomed exercise. Pippa put up a hare and set off in pursuit. Honey, busy with her thoughts, ignored the breach of discipline. She could see no easy way, for the moment, of discovering whether the Doctor was in the habit of interfering with his female patients. It was not the kind of subject that either party would openly discuss, and she had a feeling that the dividing line between examination and interference might be a rather hazy one.

She was in need of an outspoken lady who had fallen out with the Doctor.

It would not be difficult to find out what testimony he had given in recent court cases. But this, she could see, was merely continuing the hit-or-miss method which might have a one in a hundred chance of connecting within the next ten years. She began again to seethe at having been set an impossible task. Instead of a known crime, she had been offered a known culprit with the whole gamut of criminal law available to provide possible explanations for his conduct. This upside-down approach to criminal investigation would demand more than the usual resources, but even those inadequate resources were simply unavailable. Failing a lucky break or a stroke of genius, she was doomed to failure. Having seen Mr Blackhouse at work, she was aware that in the event of any complaint or criticism her period in favour might evaporate like morning dew, leaving her exposed and vulnerable; she must therefore keep a clear record in secret but available, and be able to show that she had done everything possible in impossible circumstances. Her only comfort was that Mr Blackhouse, after handing her a task that he had been told to forget about, could hardly bring disciplinary proceedings against her if she ignored his commands.

Looking down the hill, her eye was drawn to where she had met the Doctor. What exactly had his attitude been when he spoke of Honey's husband being in the police? Had there been a trace of guilt? She thought not. Recalling his apparent openness, the slight closure at the corners of his eyes and a lift at the corners of his mouth, she thought that he had been amused. But this was in retrospect. It would be easy to project any expression onto the remembered face. And if he had shown amusement had it been the amusement of the innocent man imagining the police pursuing the guilty and passing him by? Or was it the secret laughter of the guilty ... the fox watching the hounds go past? She wished that she could live the moment over again.

She was roused from her reverie by a snuffling close to her ear. Wilbur, a retired Clydesdale horse, was stretching over the trough to remind her of his presence. She produced the apple and was reminded again of the softness of a horse's lips, mumbling against her palm. She already had a rough, flexible plan of action. She pushed herself up, gave Wilbur a pat on the neck and started back.

Pippa returned to join her. At a range of twenty paces, it became obvious that she had once again rolled in something that smelled of rotting silage but this time with overtones of diesel oil and something long dead. There was no point being angry; dogs have little concept of cause-and-effect and the bitch would not understand her anger at what, to Pippa, was a natural action aimed at concealing her own scent from a predator or prey. She held the lead at arm's length and set off for home.

Kate had returned to her window and was making signals. Honey made signs to convey *Soon*. She also pointed at Pippa and held her nose. June was usually willing to bath Pippa, but not when Honey had behaved in a way that June deemed inappropriate, as for instance in going for walks when in an advanced state of pregnancy. But having to bend down and use both hands was just as unacceptable to Honey. She gave Pippa a spray with biological animal deodorant and hoped for the best. To improve the chances of avoiding domestic friction she shut Pippa in the back porch that served as her bedroom, leaving the window wide open. She washed her hands, changed her shoes and crossed the street.

Kate Ingliston opened the door as she arrived and welcomed her into the clean-smelling hall. During the week, Kate might present an imperfect image to the world; but she was an excellent housekeeper. She had the help of a local woman for two mornings a week, but that degree of help was not enough to explain the immaculate cleanliness of her house and fabrics, the polish of her furniture and the cordon *bleu* preparations for her occasional dinner parties.

When Honey was comfortably established in a chair high enough in the seat for comfort and easy entry and exit, Kate fetched coffee – of a perfection that neither Honey nor June had quite been able to achieve – and a plate of exquisite little cakes. While Kate was out of the room, Honey started the little tape recorder in her handbag. The small microphone could be mistaken for part of the fastening, if anyone bothered to look so closely. 'You and June will have me as fat as a pig if you go on feeding me like this,' Honey told her friend.

'You're eating for two and, anyway, you're one of the lucky, naturally lean ones. You have the sort of figure that snaps back into shape while other women are still several sizes larger than they were before they forgot to take their pill. Help yourself.'

Thus loudly encouraged, Honey treated herself to several of the delights. She was hungry. Despite Honey's last words, June's idea of the perfect pregnancy regime was healthy rather than filling and was based on the supposition that her mistress would rest on the sitting room couch when not actually abed. She made a show of looking out of the big sash-and-case window. 'Sometimes I see a housekeeper sort of person at the Doctor's house,' she said. 'Is she permanent or part-time? June may need some help when the baby comes and I'm back at work.'

'She's permanent,' said Kate. 'She lives in. I know because Mrs Deakin – the woman you're talking about – used to come to me part time until her husband got run over by a boat.'

'How–?'

'It was on a trailer and he didn't know that it was there and he went to cross over behind the car. Anyway, she's a widow with no family so that a live-in post was perfect for her. She might be able to spare you a little time if the Doctor doesn't mind.'

'So now the Doctor knows all your little secrets without even having to take you on his panel?'

'Oh no.' Kate sounded quite shocked. She even lowered her voice. 'She's very discreet. When she came to me she'd been working for the Harrison-Hargreaves – you may remember their divorce, or was it before your time here? Anyway, it hit the headlines locally and although I suppose it was pretty tame stuff for the London papers it fairly set this town abuzz, you'd hardly believe the carry-on – transvestism and bondage and I don't know what – and while the two main parties were hurling the details at each other in open court Mrs Deakin still wouldn't say a word about it, just turned a bit pink and went around with a secret smile on her face.'

Honey had been probing to discover whether Mrs Deakin was capable of discretion. She was not quite sure what sort of informant she was after – a close-mouthed one who would never divulge having been approached or a gossip who would spill everybody's secrets. She supposed that she would have to take whichever she could get. 'And there are no signs of a new lady in the Doctor's life?' she asked, 'But, of course, if he's lost his sex drive he may not be interested...'

'That doesn't follow at all,' said Kate.

'That he's lost it, I mean.' She pretended to look shocked. She lowered her voice to a level that was barely louder than Honey's. 'What we were saying earlier started me thinking and I could see that a man who had, let's say, used himself up for the moment with what they call a "bit on the side" might pretend to his wife that he'd gone impotent in order to cover up for a sudden loss of interest in her.'

'That's a point.' Honey said. She kept her tone light and frivolous, playing the gossiping housewife and very definitely not the investigating officer. 'I'll have to bear that in mind if Sandy ever fails to perform or pretends to have been smitten with impotence.' Honey hesitated. Sandy had seemed rather less affectionate recently, but he was probably working too hard. She hurried on. 'Have you seen any signs of a "bit on the side"? Visitors coming and going after dark? Or the Doctor slipping out at strange hours?'

Kate shook her head regretfully. 'I can't say that I have but, on the other hand, if I did I wouldn't know it. I mean, Dr Mc-Gordon has his surgery hours at the health centre and that includes evening surgeries. And he gives his services free, so I'm told, at another clinic in a very depressed part of the city; which is very good of him because it can't be very pleasant ministering to people who may not be the most orderly citizens nor too careful about personal hygiene, let alone the service being unpaid, and they say that he's very good about visiting his patients if they land in hospital, so he's coming and going all the time and nothing to say where he's been.'

'They make him sound like a saint,' said Honey. 'Who is this "they" who passes on all these details?'

'People.' Kate shrugged, laughing. 'Sometimes I meet a few old friends for coffee down at the Bridges, but three of them have gone off on a winter cruise just now, and Mary Higgins – do you know her? – she's a patient of the Doctor's and her husband plays golf with Phil, so we meet up for a meal or a drink or two now and again and she's full of his praises, the Doctor's I mean, too much so to be his "bit on the side" because – have you noticed? – a married woman with a lover never says anything good about the lover but pretends either to hate him or not to have noticed him at all, and anyway I'm afraid she's a very long way from being a man trap, what with buck teeth and a squint, they say that her husband married her for her money, so you're wrong there, she couldn't be the Doctor's new bit of stuff.'

'I never suggested that she was,' Honey said, laughing. 'In fact I never suggested that the Doctor had a ladyfriend, I only asked if there were any signs of one. And I don't even know Mary Higgins.'

'Haven't you met her? I'll invite you to meet her next time she's coming here; we were at school together, but I'll give you a tip – never ask after her health or she'll whip out her X-rays and you'll never get away.'

'I'll remember,' Honey said.

The evening rush hour starts early in Edinburgh. It was well established when Honey started for home, but she was lucky. The gaps in the traffic created by two sets of lights coincided and she made it safely across to her own side of the street. There was an unfamiliar motorcycle parked beside her Range Rover and she was pleasantly surprised to discover that PC Dodson had come to report and, unasked, had begun the process of cleansing Pippa again. Honey waited until the shower bath was finished and Pippa had given herself a good shake before revealing her return. The nearly dry bitch was shut in the back porch with a fan heater.

Dodson, profiting from what had gone before, had managed to remain almost completely dry. Honey took this as a sign that he was capable of learning by experience. She took him into the study and played him the tape of her visit to Kate Ingliston.

'That's you brought up to date,' she said. 'Now tell me all.'

Dodson nodded. He looked out of the window while he arranged his recollections. Dr McGordon's house was dark except for one window on the ground floor, but further down the street lights were coming on in the shops and houses. The street lighting was already at work. Honey was pleased to see that Dodson had committed nothing to writing. A policeman can be ordered to produce his pocket-book. There would be time enough later for making notes, once they had decided what they were prepared to divulge.

'For a start,' he said, 'if the Doctor had a hit-and-run, it seems it wasn't in his own car. I looked in the Yellow Pages for the nearest car body repairer and it's the one you said you used yourself, Lothian Coachwork, but they'd never had any plum-coloured Daimlers in for repair, not for years. So I phoned the Daimler agents and asked who they usually recommend and they referred me to Acheson Motors in Corstorphine. The young lady in the office was very discreet but I chatted her up and told her a joke or two and she loosened up. I said that we were looking for a Daimler that might have been in an accident and she told me about dents and scratches that couldn't possibly have come from a hit-and-run. There was a car that was written off, Burgundy it was, but that was a vintage Daimler Century.'

Honey decided that if Dodson had the knack of charming secretaries into unveiling records, it would be a talent worth exploiting at a later date. 'Well, we can't win 'em all,' she said. 'I'll go on following up fraud. The best thing you can do is to get onto the Internet and print off a list of the death certificates the Doctor and his partners have written, going back five years for the moment. Can you manage that?'

'Do they put death certificates on the Internet?'

'They're filed and accessible. The address of the website is in my addresses file. You'd be surprised how often death certificates need to be scrutinised.'

Dodson thought about that. 'I don't know that I would,' he said at last. 'No problem,

Inspector. But there's one more thing.' Dodson hesitated, showing embarrassment. Honey wondered what ghastly revelation was to come. Had he exposed their interest in the Doctor? Or been caught *in flagrante delicto*, doing the wrong sort of bodywork on top of the filing cabinet with the receptionist at Acheson Bodywork? But apparently not. 'I have another line of enquiry, Inspector, but it would be ... frowned on. Do you want to know?'

Honey understood immediately. She had been caught in the same kind of quandary herself. 'Dodson,' she said seriously, 'I very much want not to know, at least not yet. When the time comes that you have to tell me, so be it. Until then, I may as well be able to say that I don't know what you're up to. If you have a good line of enquiry, which might get you into trouble, it's up to yourself whether you pursue it. Later, I may be able to obtain the same information again by legitimate means and get it into evidence. There's no pressure on you and if it backfires I would try to help you, provided that it hasn't entailed murder or more than a little blackmail, but how much help I could be I just don't know. The way that these things usually turn out is that if it doesn't work and you're caught, your name is mud; but if it succeeds there's a lot of nodding and winking and the whisper goes round that you're a good lad and well worth watching. And this conversation never happened. You follow me?'

'All the way, Mrs Laird.' His tone gave no hint as to whether he was going ahead or would drop that line of enquiry like the hot potato that it almost certainly was.

## Chapter Six

Sandy had been caught up in a developing case and did not get home until Honey was already in bed and had fallen into a deep sleep. He slipped very gently in beside her and placed a soft kiss on her neck. She might have turned cold but she was still the mother of his future child and he loved her dearly.

They met at breakfast. Sandy had carried his plate and cup into the study where he was looking over his papers for the coming day in court. Honey was still in her pyjamas and a silk dressing gown that she had bought on her honeymoon. Sandy was smartly dressed and ready to go.

Instead of a kiss he greeted her with, 'June tells me that you've been going for walks.'

Honey's face fell. Instead of offering her lips she turned away. 'Only a little way up the farm track. I'm perfectly fit for that.' She raised her voice to carry to the kitchen. 'And if June's going to clype on me, I'm going to be a lot less accommodating about sudden afternoons off whenever her boyfriend phones.'

Sandy laughed. 'Fair's fair. She always tells you if I've taken my golf clubs in the car.'

Honey was ready with a heartfelt answer for that one. 'Usually that means that you're going for ten minutes of practice on the driving range. In fact, I wish you'd take a little more time off and relax. You're not getting the fresh air and exercise that you need. And no more am I.'

Sandy nodded. It was some comfort that she was still giving thought to his health and well-being. She had scored her point and should be left to enjoy it. 'I hope you're carrying your mobile. There may be a precedent for a baby boy to be born in a manger but I want my daughter to make her debut in hospital.'

'So do I.' Honey showed him her mobile

and slipped it back into her pocket. 'Did you manage to do what I asked you?'

Sandy's hand paused halfway to his mouth with toast and marmalade. 'Some of it. Now that most of the old records have been computerised it's become a lot easier, provided that they haven't got lost in the process. I suggested Dr McGordon's name to the computer and got several immediate reactions. He seems to have a short fuse and a short memory. As a student, he got into trouble over drinking sprees and one case of filling his old banger with fuel and driving away without paying. But that was a long time ago and that incident may have been the merest absentmindedness although the magistrate didn't think so. As to the rest, we all know what medical students are. More recently, he got involved in a road rage punch-up. The Doctor's a tougher character than he looks, and he looks a bit of a hard case. The other man came off decidedly worse and spent some time in hospital, but it was felt, on rather slender grounds and bearing in mind McGordon's status as a doctor, that there had been elements of provocation and self-defence.'

His voice faded. Honey looked at her husband sharply. 'There's something else, isn't

83

there? I can tell.'

'Nothing hard or fast.' Sandy hesitated. 'I'll mention this in absolute confidence. It's very strictly need-to-know.'

Honey wondered if he was angling to be coaxed and petted into disgorging the information. If so, he was going to be out of luck. 'I can keep a secret. Get on with it,' she said.

'All right. But just bear in mind that this is the sort of thing that's never said aloud. We like people to believe that it never happens. I'd have preferred that you didn't know, because you do sometimes claim the moral high ground.'

There might be some truth in that allegation but Honey would have preferred it to join whatever else was not to be said aloud. 'Get on with it,' she said again.

Sandy sighed. He had been hoping for a little gentle persuasion but it seemed that whatever had got up Honey's nose was still lodged in that attractive organ. 'All right. The Doctor does a great deal of good. He gives his services free in poor areas. He spends vacations in underdeveloped countries, helping out in free clinics. He has even been known to bring patients back to Britain at his own expense for special treatments not available elsewhere. For that reason, he's allowed a little latitude.' Sandy lowered his voice. 'He has some powerful friends, but you already know that. There's a suspicion that the Doctor drives occasionally while slightly under the influence, but his actual driving has never been at fault. General opinion is that even when he's had a few drams he's still a better driver than many another man stone-cold sober.'

'What are you saying?'

'There's no instruction given. Traffic police have been allowed to understand – it's no stronger than that – that unless he's definitely overstepped the mark and seems to be a danger to the public, which has never happened yet, the turning of a blind eye now and again will be considered acceptable.'

'Now that,' Honey said, 'is just dandy.' She also dropped her voice. The walls were thick but sound sometimes penetrated through the hatch. 'So I'm supposed to investigate a short-tempered drunk of questionable honesty, who's so well thought of that he can flout the law, and all without letting him know that he's under investigation.'

'That's about it,' her husband agreed. 'I know you find life boring if it gets too easy. And there's one other snippet. I had a word with a lawyer – nobody you'd know – and he agrees that Dr McGordon does sometimes give evidence.'

'Shaken Baby Syndrome?' Honey asked hopefully.

'Industrial injuries. He's going to look out a few cases.'

Honey made a grunt of disappointment. Industrial injuries might be a more fertile area for biased evidence and corruption but evidence of bias or corruption would be much more difficult to prove. 'If you're in the factory this morning, how would you like to make and take a phone call for me?'

'I would have been charmed. But I'm giving evidence of arrest in Glasgow. Arrested here for an assault in Barrowland. A total waste of time, but the motions have to be gone through.' Sandy planted a quick peck on her cheek before she could turn it away and made his usual hurried exit.

Honey glanced at the clock. Prue Bishop would not be at her desk yet. Later in the morning she would find it possible to do her phoning from the office and call in at the birthing classes for which she had been enrolled and which she had never so far managed to attend. She had never believed it worthwhile to anticipate an approaching discomfort. Dentist's appointments lurked forgotten until her computer told her that the day had arrived. Without thinking much about the ordeal to come, she was satisfied that a thousand generations of women had managed to continue the species. The fact that a large percentage of women went on to have a second and even a third baby suggested that it could not be as painful as portrayed by a host of film actresses. The present state of medical science made the process relatively safe and no more painful than it had to be, but a token visit to the classes might appease her many would-be nursemaids.

It seemed opportune to open her email. She booted up and signed in. Once she had managed to eradicate a host of advertisements from her service provider, an announcement from her supermarket of forthcoming bargains, several charity solicitations and an offer of pornography at discount prices, she was left with three serious communications; the newsy letter from an old friend in Monaco she filed for later attention; her father acknowledged her email and had started tactful enquiries; and there was an email from Canada to the effect that the Doctor's sister-in-law frequently had

friends and relations staying. Dulcie Mc-
Gordon might well have moved on, even
married again and changed her name. A
good photograph would enable proper but
discreet enquiries to be made.

A photograph might be near to impossible. Asking around in the hope of finding a
snapshot would probably cause a storm.
Perhaps an Identikit... But even that pre-
sented problems. She had only seen Dulcie
McGordon in the distance and far from
recently. She shook her head, closed down
the computer and called down a curse on
the head of Detective Superintendent
Blackhouse. It was far from the first such
damnation that she had uttered, but it
seemed that Somebody Up There was not
listening. It was yet another reason to
disbelieve in a personal God.

She found June in the kitchen, ironing
shirts. June's usually sunny face looked
sulky. Honey had seen the same expression
on the face of an arrestee who was just
deciding to make a groundless complaint of
police brutality. 'You're not really going to
be difficult when I want time off?' June
asked. 'My Jim never knows when his free
days are going to be changed. And I always
make up the time.' She passed a vicious iron

over one of Sandy's shirts.

'Of course you do,' Honey said, lowering her weight into a chair. 'And I'm not going to be difficult, not unless you go running to the boss every time I go for a stroll up the farm track. Let's just try to be helpful to each other.'

June thought it over and then nodded. 'All right.'

'Start with this, then. And, mind, this is very confidential. You know Mrs Deakin next door?'

June folded the shirt, made another pass with the iron and laid both aside. 'Not to say know. We've said "Good morning" over the wall a time or two and maybe said that it was hot or cold or too windy to hang out the washing. She seems a pleasant enough body but keeps herself to herself.'

'Could you get to know her better?'

'Aye. Likely. I've had the feeling that she's maybe a bit lonely but didn't want to be the first to open up. I felt the same but I had my next date with Jim to look forward to and I've family not so far away. I thought you might not like me bringing the neighbour's staff into your house,' June added in a tone of conscious virtue.

'Bring anybody you like in, as long as it's

in your part of the house and they're clean, sane and sober; I thought that that was understood. It's this way,' Honey said. 'The Doctor may be a perfectly respectable gentleman, but the question has been raised that he may have some guilty secret. We don't know what or life would be very much easier, but we'd be just as happy to find that he's perfectly innocent as we would be to find that he's up to no good. And he is not to know that he's being looked into, that's important. I'm sure you can see what a difference it would make if we had somebody gathering gossip on the inside.'

June pursed her lips. 'It's important?'

'We don't even know whether it's important or a nothing. We only know that the Doctor showed signs of feeling guilty about something serious but we don't know what. I can only say that if it's nothing then there's no need for anybody to be hurt.'

'That seems sensible. I'll help if I can,' June said. She'd already brightened at the prospect of being included in her employers' investigations, which she always looked on as having a special glamour, combining as they did mystery with the scales of justice, added to which was the awe with which her present boyfriend, who occupied a much lower rung on the same ladder, spoke of the senior officers.

'Without giving the game away? I'm sure you can manage that,' Honey said. 'And if you come up with anything really useful...' Honey paused and thought. It went against the grain to offer a monetary reward out of her own pocket for a task that she should never have been landed with in the first place. It might even prove to be the thin end of the wedge. 'An extra week's holiday with free accommodation on Crete.' The family owned several shares in a timeshare on Crete and it was often standing empty. If they were getting free accommodation, Jim could pay the fares.

'There's one other thing,' Honey added. 'If you can get hold of a photograph of Mrs McGordon without starting anybody thinking, that would be a huge help.'

During the enforced period of bed-rest, Honey had half forgotten how to drive and everything in the Range Rover had been adjusted to suit June and the weekly shopping. First she had to reposition the seat to make room for the bump and to allow for her disinclination to fold in the middle. Then she had to gather her wits and remind herself of the various moves to be made. The

Range Rover had an automatic gearbox but it was still necessary to coordinate various movements of the hands and feet while watching the movements of traffic, pedestrians and animals. The knack of driving on autopilot seemed to have deserted her. She had to think about what she was doing. Some activities are so dependent on the response of the reflexes that they become more difficult if subjected to conscious thought; happily, for Honey, driving was not one of them. She kept her mind on the vehicle and the road and, although Edinburgh rush hours get ever longer, there is still a lull in mid-morning and again in the early afternoon. She arrived unscathed at Police HQ ('the factory', as it is known to most of its occupants), parked with a dry mouth and carried a cup of coffee to her desk. Some minutes were wasted in assuring colleagues that she was fit, that the gestation was proceeding to plan and that she was only in the office to make and receive a phone call, before she could get down to that task.

Prue answered the phone and there followed the inevitable interval of baby talk – a subject of which Honey was becoming heartily morning-sick. Only Sandy, it seemed, ever wanted to talk to her about anything else and he had not been very forthcoming of late. They disconnected and Prue called back immediately. Evidently the switchboard constituted a satisfactory identification. 'All right,' Prue said. 'Now that I know that you are who you say you are, I've prepared an email with what you wanted.'

Honey gave her home email address. They exchanged more good wishes and broke the connection. The email, Honey thought, had better contain some gems of information after so much time and trouble. She set off to return to her Range Rover.

It was with mixed feelings that she found herself alone in the lift with Detective Superintendent Blackhouse. On the one hand, he was quite her least favourite person in the whole world; on the other, the encounter afforded her a chance to show by her manner how little she appreciated being handed impossible tasks during what should have been her time for rest and the thinking of pure and beautiful thoughts. It would be the Superintendent's fault, she thought, if her baby's first sight of the world entailed darting suspicious glances at it from the corners of her eyes.

Mr Blackhouse, however, was not in a mood for noticing the body language of his subordinates. 'What are you doing here?' he demanded. 'You're supposed to be at home. I was about to phone you there.'

Honey was surprised by this evidence of consideration in one who usually cared little for the health or comfort of his juniors. He must be concerned for his future godchild. 'I'm quite all right,' she said. 'I just had to come in to take a phone call.'

The Superintendent was magnificently uninterested. 'You'd better hurry back straight away. Somebody is waiting to get in touch with you with some significant information.' And with that, the lift pausing at his floor, he stepped outside and the doors closed again. Honey was left to wonder whether a rude answer, a quick resignation and acceptance of the role of wife and mother would really have been such a terrible outcome.

## Chapter Seven

Habits, once contracted, are rarely quite forgotten. Honey's old habit patterns had made their comeback. She found herself able to drive again without conscious thought. She carved her way through the early lunchtime traffic without even being aware of it. The downside to this was that her mind was free to notice the bodily discomfort of sitting in just the wrong position and making movements that did not go well with her expanding condition. She decided that she would please her nannies by refusing to drive herself in future. The time for her appointment at the birthing clinic had arrived and would soon be gone, but they would just have to get by without her and she without them.

'You didn't tell me when you'd be back,' was June's greeting.

'I didn't *know* when I'd be back,' Honey retorted gently.

'You're supposed to be at the birthing clinic.'

'I was on my way there when a very, very important officer, senior even to Mr Sandy, told me to scoot back here because somebody has some information for me.'

June backed up against the coats to let her past and then followed her to the sitting room door. Her face showed relief and enlightenment. She produced a slip of paper. 'This'll be what it's about. There was a lady phoned, asking. You're to call this number, urgent.' June's abruptness was explained. It had been drummed into her that the passing on of messages was a sacred duty and that death was the only possible excuse for failure or even delay.

Honey took the slip of paper into the study. The number looked faintly familiar. The phone at the other end had time for only one ring before it was lifted. A female voice quoted the same number. Honey introduced herself by no more than her married name. 'Please stay at home,' the voice said. 'We'll be with you in a few minutes.' The entire conversation had occupied barely five seconds. For a completed exchange between two women, Honey thought, it must be worth a place in the *Guinness Book of Records*. Between men, it would be considered about average. She had no illusions about the garrulity of her own sex.

It seemed to be a safe assumption that this person, lone or accompanied, was the informant promised by the Superintendent and therefore could be presumed to be safe. Honey arranged her tape recorder under the coffee table again. When, after ten minutes, the doorbell rang she started the recording and waited while June answered the door.

'The two ladies, Ma'am,' June said. 'They wouldn't give me their names.'

'Tea please, June.'

'I shan't be staying for more than a minute,' the younger visitor said.

'Perhaps not,' Honey said. 'But you'd think it very odd if I ordered tea but left you out. Nobody says that you have to drink it. But I think I know who you are anyway. Please sit down.'

The visitors sat. 'There's no secret about my identity,' the younger visitor said. 'I simply mustn't be associated with this business. As you seem to be aware, I'm Mrs Blackhouse.'

Honey managed to hide her surprise, but it took an effort. She had seen the blonde woman in the distance, dancing attendance on the Superintendent at some of the more formal social occasions, but without any likelihood of being introduced. She had assumed that any woman of around thirty – at least twenty years younger than the Superintendent and with more than her fair share of sex appeal and all the signs of youthful good humour – would have to be a daughter rather than a wife. Or a daughter-in-law? Mr Blackhouse had never been forthcoming about his family.

She was not a daughter-in-law. 'My husband asked me to bring Felicia Aston to meet you. You may have seen her visiting the house next door.' This was said with a meaningful look.

'Not that I ever noticed,' Honey said; 'but I can be very unobservant at times.' She returned the look with a nod. Understanding had been exchanged.

'I'll leave you to it,' Mrs Blackhouse said. 'I'm not to join in any discussions at all – my husband was very clear about that. I'll leave Felicia with you. You'll see that she gets home?'

'Of course.'

'I'll see myself out.'

They heard the front door close behind her. A car started and was driven away. It seemed that Mr Blackhouse's word was as much law at home as among his subordinates. June arrived with the tea-tray and noted the disappearance of one guest with no more reaction than a raised eyebrow and carried away the surplus cup. Since being admitted into the inner circle of investigators, June seemed to be coming to accept that normality no longer had quite the same force.

Mrs Aston (Honey noticed rings on her finger, including a good diamond and ruby engagement ring) spoke for the first time. She looked around. 'I like what you've done with this room,' she said. 'I don't call that much of an introduction, but Gemma was always the hasty one. As you've gathered, I'm Felicia Aston. And you're Mrs Laird?'

'Honoria, usually known as Honey.'

Mrs Aston half rose and reached to shake hands. Like Mrs Blackhouse, she was aged around thirty but slightly the older of the pair. She was a larger than average woman but well proportioned. Her clothes were expensive, conventional and disciplined. Her auburn hair was styled elegantly but firmly. Although her face was equally well proportioned and could have been beautiful, a strong jaw and a proud nose robbed it of femininity and gave it a look of almost masculine strength. While Mrs Blackhouse had looked as though she might be firm, Mrs Aston, once she made up her mind, would be immoveable. Her dress was conventional, unexceptionable and expensive.

'Now that we've introduced ourselves,' Mrs Aston said, 'perhaps you could tell me why I'm here.'

'I only have a vague idea as to why you're here,' Honey said. She decided to tread warily. 'But I'm sure that I can work it out if you tell me what led up to it.'

Mrs Aston shrugged, rather elegantly. 'I

suppose. I've known Gemma Blackhouse since Day One – we were at school together. We make a point of meeting up sometimes. Well, it's only too rare for the husbands of friends to get on with each other just as well as their wives do. But then, Josh Blackhouse is a lovely man, isn't he?'

Honey forced herself to nod and smile. They surely couldn't be talking about any other Blackhouse. She wondered what sort of woman would think him lovely. There were many other words that she could have applied to the Superintendent but none of them carried the same meaning. She wondered what facet of his appearance or nature was under consideration. Honey could only assume that the Detective Superintendent had an alternative personality to be switched on only on social occasions.

'We met for dinner last night,' Mrs Aston resumed, 'the Blackhouses, my husband and I and another couple. And Josh said that he wanted me to speak to you.'

'What direction had the conversation been taking?' Honey asked.

Mrs Aston accepted tea and a small cake. She looked at her perfect fingernails while she considered. 'Mostly we'd been talking about the mess the NHS is getting into and particularly how lucky you'd have to be to get referred from your own area to where the best treatment is or where the more expensive drugs get prescribed. We knew a man who gave up his job and moved house into an inner-city area to give his wife the best chance of surviving cancer of the pancreas. And as for transplants... You can beat the system and go private, but the cost is phenomenal.'

'What else?' Honey prompted her.

'That was most of it. The men talked rugby and the women talked clothes.'

'Mrs Blackhouse said something about next door.'

Mrs Aston's proud nose went up. 'I only came to his house once, to collect a prescription, although he does see patients here when it suits him. But I mentioned that I'd been a patient of Dr McGordon. I switched to one of his partners about a year ago and left to register with a different practice quite recently.'

Honey felt the need to walk ever more gently. 'That would be so that there could be no objection to an increasing friendship?'

The other looked at her sharply. 'Are you a friend of his?'

That told Honey what she needed to

know. 'Certainly not. Are you?'

'Good God no! I can't stand the man. He's a damn good doctor with a well run practice, but I left him and then his practice to get away from him. If you're thinking of consulting him, you may be getting a good doctor but...'

'But?'

Mrs Aston showed a trace of embarrassment unsuited to her strong features. 'This is just between ourselves?'

'I promise. If we need to make further use of anything you tell me now, we'll get back to you for a fresh statement.'

Mrs Aston thought it over and seemed to find it acceptable. 'How to put it into words? There's no accounting for likes and dislikes, even for mistrust. Feelings can't be spelled out. I conceived a dislike of the Doctor.' Her white skin took on a dusky hue. 'I went to him with a mild skin condition. His diagnosis was clearly accurate and his prescription cleared it up straight away. What was just as clear was that he could have arrived at the same diagnosis and treatment without making me undress. In point of fact, I think he'd made up his mind the moment I walked through the door. He had a nurse present, of course, but I knew, the way one does, that he was laughing at me. What was worse, he was getting... You know?'

'He fancied you?' Honey said, carefully unsmiling.

Mrs Aston's jaw took on an angrier tilt and her plucked eyebrows seemed to bristle. 'He was getting randy, I could tell. When a man gets both randy and amused, you can be sure that he's fantasising all sorts of things that you'd rather not know about.' She paused and there was a moment of silence. 'I'm speaking for myself. Some women may enjoy being lusted after or even being the subject of erotic fantasies, but it does less than nothing for me. So now, what's this about? Is it true that you're a detective?'

There was no danger that Felicia Aston would hurry to warn the Doctor that he was being investigated. 'I'm a detective inspector,' Honey said. 'I'm usually part of Mr Blackhouse's team. We have some reason to believe that the Doctor has something on his conscience. We don't know what. Because I live next door, I've been asked to while away the remainder of my pregnancy in finding out. There may be nothing or it may be trivial, but we have to look into these things; and because he has some important people among his patients and possibly among his friends, it has to be done very discreetly.'

Mrs Aston's face relaxed. The expression of anger and contempt was replaced by one of mild satisfaction. 'I see that. And I won't say a word. I'll help all I can, but I'll tell you this; most of his patients are men. Women don't stay long on his panel, but I've never heard of any behaviour that would cause the GMC to look at him sideways, nothing that you could put your finger on. Damn!' she added. 'I made up my mind that I wasn't going to say that.'

Honey couldn't help it. Her always rather ribald sense of humour took over. She smiled and a small snort of laughter escaped her. Felicia Aston's formidable self-control slipped and she chuckled. Honey laughed aloud and in a moment the two were giggling together like schoolgirls. When the moment had passed, Honey wiped her eyes with a tissue and said, 'Anything that you can tell me, anything at all, might be a help towards deciding, is there something worth investigating or isn't there?'

The smile quite gone, Mrs Aston regarded Honey solemnly. 'I'll help if I can, as I said, but I warn you that I don't know much about the man. My reaction to him is a gut reaction, nothing more. Perhaps it's to do with telepathy. Socially, he gets accepted as a friendly, hearty man-about-town. More, I think, by men than women. As a doctor my husband can't see anything wrong with him, but when his name comes up among women there's a moment of silence and then one or two say that they think he's marvellous and they talk about the services that he gives for nothing in Bosnia and places like that. But the others must have picked up the same vibrations that came to me. They either damn him with faint praise or make the sort of comments that don't mean much on their own but add up to something nasty. One friend of mine, when we were alone together and she'd had a couple of gins, said that she was sure that, while he was being very helpful and professional, he secretly thought of her as a large, walking vulva with sagging tits. Have I shocked you?'

'I am a detective inspector,' Honey reminded her. 'I've heard much worse, often.'

The other looked surprised. 'I suppose that's true. You must get used to seeing people at their worst, like dentists and social workers. And then there's his nephew. Thank God I never needed surgery.' Honey must have looked puzzled. 'Didn't you know? He has a nephew, Andrew Samson, a surgeon, who goes with him on his charitable trips. He works at one of the NHS hospitals but moonlights at a private clinic. If you go to Dr McGordon and need anything in the field of general surgery, that's where you'll be sent. Perfectly competent but, from what I hear, they're each as bad as the other. Mister – one must call a surgeon Mister, mustn't one? Mr Samson's said to be a very good surgeon. And I know that he's a brilliant anaesthetist, because a friend of my husband's had to have a growth removed from his face. They brought in a specialist and Mr Samson gave the anaesthetic. George – our friend – said that he never even knew that he'd been out; he was chatting with the nurses when he realised that they were wheeling him back to the ward. He asked why he wasn't getting his operation and they told him that he'd just had it. It wasn't until the painkillers began to wear off that he believed them.

'On the other hand, Mr Samson's just built himself a very expensive house to the east of Edinburgh and he shouldn't be able to afford that sort of thing when he's not long out of the egg, surely? I mean, there's no money in that family except for his uncle's earnings and he didn't marry money. Quite the reverse. One of my oldest friends lives next door to them and she says that his wife spends money as though it can give you acne if you keep it around for too long.'

'Go on,' Honey said, smiling.

Mrs Aston had smiled again but now she frowned. For a moment, she could have been sitting at the foot of the guillotine. 'I think I've said most of it. Professionally, Dr McGordon's damn good, but I don't know anything beyond what I've seen of him, going to his clinic, being examined–' she gave a ladylike shudder '–and diagnosed and prescribed. What goes on behind the scenes I wouldn't know, but I think I know who you should be talking to. A neighbour of mine, Marjory Allen, was his receptionist and bookkeeper for years. As you say, he may be pure as the driven snow, at least in the eyes of the law and the GMC. If there's the least chance that he isn't, I'd want to help bring it out. Shall I fix up a meeting for coffee somewhere?'

'Why not here?'

Felicia Aston considered and then shook her head. 'I think not. Your problem is that she still thinks that Dr McGordon is the best thing since the Pill. Does that matter?'

'Not in the least,' Honey said. 'What friends *say* is often just as revealing as what enemies say, and usually closer to the truth.'

107

'I suppose that's so. But it means that if we ask her here, she'll wonder why. A chance meeting in a neutral place might do it. I'll phone you.'

'That will be fine,' Honey said, 'but make it soon. I may not be out and about for much longer. Before you go, did you know the Doctor's wife?'

'Yes, I knew Dulcie. A love-hate relationship, I always thought. I wasn't surprised when she ran off. If that's what happened...' She looked at Honey with her eyes wide.

We don't have the faintest idea,' Honey said. 'But it would help if we had a photograph of Dulcie McGordon.'

'I bet it would. And I think you may be in luck. I'll go home now and look through my box of snapshots.' She got to her feet and looked vaguely over Honey's shoulder in the direction of a pastel sketch of an unidentified landscape in a gilt frame. 'You know, it never occurred to me–'

'Please,' Honey said. 'Let's not make guesses. I'm told that Mrs McGordon went to her sister in Canada and I just want to prove that it's true. You'll keep all this between ourselves?'

'Of course. Absolutely.'

There was an uncomfortable pause. Honey

was dying to say that 'between ourselves' meant that nobody, literally nobody whatsoever, was to be told; but she had a feeling that such an admonition might put Mrs Aston's back up and that, in the process of complaining to some friend, and quite possibly that friend would be Marjory Allen, that she had been lectured like a child, the rest of the story would be spilled. Honey could only hope that Mrs Aston was a woman of her word, but it was a slender hope. There are not many of them around when it comes to confidences.

They parted on friendly terms.

## *Chapter Eight*

June was a competent driver and quite used to the Range Rover. Rather than suffer more discomfort and invite further arguments about the danger of stress and exertion causing her baby to be born exhausted and with a bad case of road rage, Honey sent Felicia Aston home in the Range Rover with June as chauffeuse, thus obtaining for herself an interval in which to open her emails.

Prue Bishop had furnished the list of GPs under audit for possible fraud on the NHS, but Dr McGordon's name and those of his partners were not among them. That, of course, did not mean that the Doctor was innocent any more than that the presence of his name would have meant that he was guilty of anything. No doubt there were many doctors who padded their list of patients or claimed time and mileage in respect of maladies dealt with over the phone; but their names would only come to the attention of the Audit Department due to some slip-up or a disaffected staff member.

Mr Potterton-Phipps emailed that the Doctor's credit was excellent, that he had no discoverable debts, always paid up on time and seemed to be a first-class financial risk. That could be a good sign or a bad one, depending on whether one took it to mean solid respectability or access to easy money. He did not seem to have fallen foul of any of Mr Potterton-Phipps's interests except that he had once given evidence in a case brought by a former employee of a subsidiary who complained that he had been left to lift a load that was too heavy for one man. Dr McGordon had given purely medical evidence calmly and dispassionately. The man

110

had won his case for compensation for his damaged back and Mr Potterton-Phipps acknowledged that the verdict was a fair one.

She logged off and took Pippa for a walk to clear her mind, but the day was dank and misty. All that could be said for it was that the clegs that had been so troublesome in summer were absent now. She kept Pippa on the lead. It was not a day for optimistic contemplation. Honey had never tried to run through knee-deep treacle, but she supposed that it might well bear a strong resemblance to trying to solve the case of an unknown offence with no resources and no starting point. She had experienced much the same sensation during her childhood while trying to walk up a dune of fine, dry, shifting sand. One step up, one slide back. It was a relief when her mobile played her a tune. It was June, to say that lunch was ready.

She rested after lunch. Dozing, she heard the telephone ring but she dived back into repose. She awoke in half an hour, feeling miserable until she had washed her face and cleaned her teeth. On her return down-stairs, June greeted her with a mug of tea and the news that Felicia Aston wanted her to call back. Her spirits dipped and then, always buoyant, rose. This could be more bad news but the balance of probabilities suggested that any news would be good.

Mrs Aston still sounded competent and in command. Her dislike of the Doctor was evident in her tone of voice whenever he was mentioned. She had met Marjory Allen in the corner shop, she said, and they had arranged to meet for coffee next day in a convenient Starbucks. And more good news. She had found a photograph that included a good likeness of Dulcie McGordon.

Even while they spoke, Honey was already turning over in her mind the steps required before a conventional photograph could be emailed. Where could she call on the sort of services usually provided by the police technicians? It struck her suddenly that a vital question remained unasked. 'Who took the photograph?'

'Roddy. My husband.'

'An ordinary camera or a digital?' Honey held her breath while awaiting reply.

'Digital.'

Honey breathed more easily. Perhaps she was beginning to get a run of luck. 'I'll have to send it by email,' she said, 'so I need to get my hands on the digital image rather than a print.'

'I'm looking at the digital image now. I

remembered the picture and scrolled through the frames in Roddy's camera until I found it. Anything that he really wants to keep he transfers to the computer and then onto a CD, but the rest he just leaves in the camera in case he ever finds a use for them. The camera can hold hundreds and hundreds of images.'

'Would you write down the number, please. It's probably in the top, right-hand corner of the digital image. To be safe, write down all the numbers that appear round the frame. Then take out the memory card or stick or whatever it is. I'll send June to collect it.' Her rather tentative resumption of driving had convinced Honey that the Range Rover, even after adjustment of the seat and the steering column, was not tailored to accommodate a lady at an advanced stage of pregnancy, nor was her own driving of it while in that condition as safe as she would have liked. June's anxiety over injury to the foetus seemed to be catching. She was learning to worry for two.

For the first time, Mrs Aston's calm assertiveness began to slip. 'I wouldn't know how to do a thing like that,' she said. 'I can just about turn it on and off and push the button.'

Honey closed her eyes for a moment.

Perhaps her spirits had risen too soon. She had forgotten how inept some people could become when taken outside their own immediate experiences. 'Can I borrow the whole camera for about half an hour?' she asked.

'I suppose that will be all right. But I must have it back before Roddy comes home.'

'You will. Cop's honour!' Honey was feeling a return of her old, flippant self. If the Doctor's fit of conscience had to do with the disposal of his wife, his sin might be about to return to haunt him.

Honey had to threaten to drive the Range Rover herself, which activity June had now convinced herself would result in the early demise of Honey and, worse, the baby, before June would agree to drive back over the ground that she had covered not long before; and that was with the proviso that Honey stood guard over June's baking, which would be certain to combust if left to itself. Honey told her to drive carefully and be sure to stop at the red lights, which she knew would annoy June but was a fair tit-for-tat after all the grannyish warnings that June had heaped on her. She spent twenty minutes composing an email reply to her friend in Monaco. When she heard the

Range Rover, she darted back to the kitchen, or as near to darting as a lady with a seriously enlarged figure could manage. The baking was perfectly all right.

Felicia Aston had provided a slip of paper with the crucial number upon it. When Honey settled down in the study and transferred the memory card to her own computer and called that frame up, she found a group of five ladies, of approximately similar age and colouring. Mrs Aston, contacted on the phone, was prepared to swear that Dulcie McGordon was the central figure, the only one with upswept hair and a blue dress. The picture was sharp and showed an attractive woman, on the plump side but still exhibiting sex appeal. Unlike the others in the group she wore no jewellery but Honey noted that her dress was expensively cut. Her hair was simply styled, shoulder length and in apparently natural waves. Her face was round and short-nosed but the consequent babyish look that is often attractive to men was wearing thin. The background scenery could have been a street of shops almost anywhere in the world.

Honey was struggling to pull the face up, clarify it and encapsulate it in an email to Canada, due to a lack of familiarity with the editing program, when she heard the drum-ming of a powerful motorcycle outside and she was saved by the arrival of Constable Dodson. She hastened to the front door to admit him and hustle him through to the study where he was soon settled at the com-puter with Honey managing to look over his shoulder despite her bump. The Constable, it transpired, was more computer literate than Honey and quite familiar with digital photo-graphy, so she kept him anchored to her computer until the email, carrying with it an excellent likeness of what she believed, in the light of old recollection and Mrs Aston's assurances, to be the face of Mrs McGordon, was on its way to Vancouver with a request that, if a supposed Mrs McGordon should still be in Vancouver, a photograph in return might settle the question for good and all. The camera was on its way back to Mrs Aston in the hands of an ever more irritable June, followed by a silent prayer that Mrs Aston had identified the correct lady. Only then did Honey turn him out of the desk chair and into the visitor's much less com-fortable one. She turned her mind to what-ever Dodson might have brought with him.

Dodson hesitated and looked uncertain. He produced several linked sheets of computer paper from an inner pocket. 'I couldn't make head nor tail of the Internet site – I think their computer must have crashed – so I went to the Registrar's office,' he said. 'There was a clerk there who wouldn't have given me the time of day. I watched until he went for his lunch and then went in again. There was a young lady left in charge and I sort of chatted her up. I had to show her how to make the computer cough up a list of death certificates signed by Dr McGordon and his partners.'

Honey wanted to ask him how he could have 'sort of' chatted up the secretary but decided that she might not appreciate the answer. 'At least you seem to have used your initiative,' she said. She hoped that initiative and charm had been all that he had used. She accepted the paper. It was a long list. 'They have a lot of elderly patients,' Dodson explained. He still showed signs of embarrassment. Surely, Honey thought, this could not be merely over having used his sex appeal on a secretary or office girl? Assuring herself that it would have been safe sex appeal, she transferred her attention to the papers. Somewhere among those names there might linger an explosive fragment, but not until she could look into the matter of legacies. The wills listed would be those of persons already deceased. How many wills, she wondered, had made favourable mention of the Doctor but were still lying in some dark cupboard or a solicitor's safe because the testator had not yet been given that fatal push?

'Anything else?'

Dodson's embarrassment increased. He took a plastic envelope from his pocket and extracted a floppy disk. 'I'll just let you have my conclusions, if you like,' he said.

'That comes later. Give me the disk.'

'You may prefer not to see it.'

'I can't tell until I've seen it. Come on. Cough it up.'

Silently and with evident embarrassment, Dodson parted with the disk. Honey removed the disk from the computer and replaced it with the new one. A few seconds of keying brought the images onto the screen. She was pained but not surprised to see that it was a printout of somebody's bank statements, without any name or account number. They seemed to stretch back over several years. The guilt of a highly illegal infringement of the Data Protection and several other Acts was now shared. But some irrational instinct insisted that she would feel less guilty if she kept her questions short.

'His?'

'Yes.'

'You?'

Dodson shook his head. 'I'm not much of a hacker.'

'Who, then?'

'I have a friend. He's good.'

'Not a cop?'

'No.'

If the truth ever came out, at least the hacker was not one of the police. She would therefore be able to argue that the disk was not evidence, since it was clearly inadmissible, but information obtained quite legitimately from a miscreant. The argument might be valid, or at least she could hope that it would be accepted. 'All right,' she said. 'Now tell me your conclusions.'

Dodson gave a sigh, apparently of relief. Honey guessed that he had half feared that she would blow her top at the very thought of obtaining evidence by unauthorised hacking. She thought that if he ever saw what sometimes went on he would probably have kittens. 'I know that I mentioned conclusions, but I was jumping ahead. I don't have any conclusions yet,' he said. 'But looking through the statements, I see a pattern. I'd see a lot more of it if I could get a look at his credit card accounts, but we haven't figured out a way to get at them, not yet. He does most of his spending by credit card and he lives well. I know that because he pays his council tax, his electricity and oil bills by monthly banker's order. Round about the turn of each month there's a payment, usually between two and three thousand which would have to be his credit card account, covering, I suppose, the shopping and the fuel for his Daimler.'

'And his housekeeper's wages,' Honey said.

'Yes. And he withdraws a couple of hundred at a time in cash. There's ample margin there for dining out at the best places, going to the theatre, perhaps a little gambling and so on. None of that seems significant.'

'But?'

'I was coming to but,' Dodson said placidly. '*But* each year in January or February he draws a large sum.'

'Skiing holiday, do you think?'

Dodson shook his head. 'I doubt it. Acheson Motors said that he leaves the Daimler there for a service at about that time each year and collects it after at least two weeks, sometimes a month or more.'

'He may be taking a rather expensive ladyfriend with him,' Honey pointed out. 'On the other hand, he may take his nephew, the surgeon. I've heard that he gives his services for free in underdeveloped countries and sometimes he brings back a needy case for surgery here, at his own expense. All of which makes him sound just a little bit too good to be true. But that could account for it.'

'I'd go along with that,' Dodson said, 'except that his expenses would be comparatively small, much smaller than the sums he takes out with him, even travelling First. And then, not long after the time when I'd expect him to be back, he makes a substantial payment into his account and most of it goes out again a few days later. Eight times in ten years, that amount was much larger than the original withdrawal.'

'Ah!' Honey said. 'Now you begin to interest me. Are there any other large deposits that don't fit the same pattern?'

'Depends what you call large and how you interpret the pattern.'

'I suppose that was too much to ask for. So, unless he was ministering to the medical needs of some oriental potentate, it sounds to me like smuggling and investment of the profit.'

Dodson's eyebrows went up. 'Drugs?' he suggested.

'No, not drugs. Why does everybody's mind fly to drugs when smuggling's mentioned? Too dangerous to everyone concerned, especially the carrier, and too easily detected by sniffer dogs. I'm thinking more about bringing back a patient with diamonds implanted somewhere behind his navel. With a reputable doctor and a surgeon bringing in a patient on a stretcher, who's going to ask a lot of nasty questions? Leave the disk with me. I'll save it to my hard drive and you'll get your disk back with something else saved over the top of it. Meanwhile, I'll try to find out who he uses as his travel agent. And well done, Dodson. What's your first name?'

'Allan, Inspector.'

'Well done, Allan.'

'What's next for me, Mrs Laird?'

Honey had opened her mouth to tell him before she realised that she did not have an idea in her head. 'Knock off now,' she said. 'We've broken enough rules for the moment. Phone me in the morning and I'll brief you.'

When she was alone, she tilted the chair back and went into another reverie. What would a doctor – two doctors – smuggle for maximum profit? And how would she find out if the market were being flooded with whatever it was? That, she realised, was just the kind of question to which Mr Potterton-Phipps could usually find the answer. She would pose it, next time that she saw him.

## Chapter Nine

Dodson went on his way – whistling cheerfully, Honey supposed, at the prospect of a clear evening with one or other of his girlfriends. Honey saved the Doctor's bank statements onto the computer, formatted the disk and overlaid it with a few of George Melly's lyric sheets, put the disk into an envelope for Dodson and then made her own study of the figures. She decided that Dodson was absolutely right. Each withdrawal or deposit was capable of an explanation in its own light, but the pattern as a whole was only susceptible to an innocent explanation of the most far-fetched sort. Early in every year there would be a large withdrawal, followed several months later by a usually much larger deposit and then a withdrawal by cheque of the larger part of it.

The implication was strong that a substantial profit came out of the initial expenditure and was subsequently invested. Other sums were deposited and withdrawn, at no particular interval.

She sank deep into a brown study of the facts and theories. She would, she decided, have undergone any suitable ordeal in order to get a look at the Doctor's tax returns – or anything else that would connect uninformative cheque numbers with identifiable payees. How, if at all, did he manage to keep the money out of the grasp of HM Inspector of Taxes? Perhaps he paid up, smiling, like a good little doctor, but she was prepared to bet against it. Perhaps he had found some useful escape route. If so, it was a road that she might like to take some day for herself.

She returned to reality with a jump, to realise that June was standing patiently beside her. June waited for a few more seconds until she could be sure that her mistress was back with her in mind as well as in body. 'Mr Sandy phoned,' she said. It had been agreed that this form of address would be a satisfactory compromise between formality and excessive familiarity. 'He'll be late back and I'm to keep him something hot.' (Honey quite understood although June's former English teacher would have ground her dentures.) 'And would you mind eating early, Ma'am, as the Doctor's out and Mrs Deakin's coming round for a cosy chat.'

'Eat how early?'

'Like now?'

Honey decided that the mild ache in her mid-section was not after all the fault of the foetus but was a symptom of hunger. 'No, I don't mind at all. I'll come now. Eat with me and I'll give you a fuller briefing.'

Honey was not often permitted the run of the kitchen. She had special fondness for the bright room with its jovially painted cupboard doors, shelves of jars and racks of equipment. The scents, even the echoes, reminded her of the kitchen of the big house in Perthshire where she had grown up. But June was entitled to her own province and considered the kitchen to be beneath the dignity of her employer and therefore her own. Only when June took her occasional holidays could Honey get free access to the kitchen and indulge her own passion for haute cuisine.

On this occasion as so often in the past, her suggestion that they eat in the kitchen was firmly overruled and they ate in the more formal dining room. Despite cheerful decoration, which included carpet and curtains that were almost gaudy, the room remained severe. This was because it housed a number of Victorian paintings, including family portraits, of too much historical or sentimental value to be disposed of and which Mr Potterton-Phipps had passed to them on semi-permanent loan, preferring not to retain them in his own house because of the gloom of the treatments and the unsavoury appearance of some of the sitters.

While waiting for the chicken and vegetable soup to cool and again between mouthfuls, Honey managed to give her briefing. 'I want to know everything about the Doctor,' she said. 'What opinion do you have so far? Is Mrs Deakin the Doctor's loyal retainer or does she resent him?'

June paused to swallow. 'I think – and it's only a thought – that she doesn't like him much.'

Honey knew that June was observant. She was also intelligent. She usually came to the right judgement of people even if she had difficulty in verbalising her thoughts. 'Why do you think that?' Honey asked.

June screwed up her face as she struggled to recall Mrs Deakin's words and manner and then to express her own reasoning. 'She speaks as if she doesn't want to look disloyal,' she said at last. 'Like me, she was taught that if somebody pays you a living, you owe them loyalty. Her voice doesn't change when she mentions the Doctor but it sounds careful and there's a hardness comes over her face. Does that make sense?'

'It makes a whole lot of sense. So it doesn't seem likely that she'll go running to the Doctor if she guesses that somebody's asking questions about him. But until you're absolutely sure of it, remember, she mustn't be made suspicious.' Honey took, savoured and swallowed a spoonful of soup while she called on her own years of experience in conducting enquiries. 'Be innocently curious rather than nosy and let a promising opportunity go by rather than be too direct. But I know I needn't tell you all this; your mother could always find out what she wanted to know without quite asking questions. All we want to know is why the Doctor seems to have a guilty conscience about something. What could be useful for that purpose would be the names of people who don't like the Doctor much. They might speak out and say something useful.

'She almost certainly knows that Sandy's a

detective inspector. The Doctor knew that much. She may not know that I'm tarred with the same brush, but it's no secret. Don't mention it unless the subject comes up.'

'Got you,' June said. She got up in order to serve delicate portions of lemon sole.

'You could mention what a nuisance we are, always burning our confidential papers in the fireplaces. Yes,' Honey added quickly as June began to protest, 'I know that we don't do that, we shred everything. But I want to know what happens to the Doctor's finished-with papers. Especially his credit card slips and accounts. I would dearly love to get a look at them and if you bring up the subject of disposal of private papers she may let slip a hint. But what might prove most interesting of all is the story of the foreign trips that he makes, early each year. Does his nephew go with him? Where do they go? What do they do? Does he ever show her his holiday snaps?

'And what about women? Do they ever visit? Has there ever been a whisper about him and a patient?'

'And that's all?' June asked. Honey thought that she was probably being ironic.

'I think so. I'll jot down a few topics that might be specially interesting. Just keep her talking about her life in the Doctor's house and it should come pouring out. If there's anybody in the world who doesn't enjoy talking about themselves, I never met them.' Honey paused and then decided to be quite open. 'I'm going to hide my tape-recorder somewhere handy. Then you won't be distracted by having to memorise everything. You'll be sitting in the fireside chairs?'

June nodded. 'It's the best place.'

'It's the best for me too.'

For most of the year the kitchen depended for warmth on the central heating. The Aga was cold. Later, with the tape recorder hidden in the oven section, the microphone went into a vase of dried flowers on the hotplate. As soon as she saw Mrs Deakin emerge from the Doctor's side door, Honey started the recording and retreated into the study. She fired up the computer but there were no emails waiting.

She was tired. Living for two seemed to make every task twice the effort. She decided that there were no useful steps to be taken except thinking and she could think as easily in her bed. She would hear Mrs Deakin leave and could go downstairs and listen to the tape. But she was asleep as soon as her ear met the pillow. Neither Mrs Deakin's departure nor Sandy's return home roused her.

Sandy paused during his preparations for bed and looked down at his sleeping wife. Even pregnant, perhaps especially while pregnant, she looked desirable. What had gone wrong? Why did she not respond? If she would only say, he could do something, anything, to set matters right.

Honey awoke refreshed and full of energy but alone. Daylight had returned. She listened. She could tell from the small domestic noises that Sandy would soon be leaving the house, so she donned slippers and her quilted dressing gown and hurried downstairs without pausing to do more than run her fingers through her hair. She thought that she probably looked as though she was wearing a fright wig.

Sandy was preparing to rise from the breakfast table. He caught one of her wrists and made as if to pull her down onto his knee. 'You look very sexy like that,' he said.

The last thing that Honey felt was sexy-looking. She resisted his pull, but if this was another road back towards their old relationship she wanted to know about it. 'How could I possibly?' she asked.

He looked at her and gave the question serious consideration. 'You always look sexy,' he said. He released her wrist. 'But just at this moment the tousled look is definitely in. That and the robe and the general air of sleepiness combine to suggest a woman after love, which unfortunately you aren't.'

'No, I'm not, am I?' Honey said. She glanced down at her bump which, while signifying the gateway to a whole new life, did seem to be a serious handicap in her present one. 'Try to come home tonight before I'm asleep. Sandy, have you heard from your lawyer friend?'

'About the Doctor's appearances in the witness box? I'm seeing him today.'

'I've heard about one case. He testified for a man who was given too heavy a load to lift. His evidence seems to have been accurate and impartial. What I'm looking for is any case in which his evidence may have been biased or even wrong.'

'Where backhanders may have passed, in fact. I'll see what I can do. Now, I must go. Take it easy. Not long now.'

Honey climbed back up the stairs, wondering what Sandy had meant. Not long to what? To parenthood? Or to a resumption of sexual relations? On consideration she hoped very much that he was alluding to both.

Dodson had arrived and was waiting in the study when Honey came down the stairs again. This time she was respectably dressed and groomed. They settled down in the study to listen to the tape of June's heart-to-heart with Mrs Deakin.

The first few minutes were taken up with the usual courtesies. There were remarks about how strange that they had lived next door to each other and never made social contact. 'I've thought of speaking to you a dozen times,' June said, 'but you always seemed quite happy on your own.'

Honey nodded. It was a good gambit.

'I can manage alone,' Mrs Deakin said. Her accent was Edinburgh, not one of the better areas but Honey soon decided that she was articulate and had been well schooled. 'But it's always better to have someone to talk with.'

Honey noticed the *talk with*. Most women would have said *talk to*.

'I know just what you mean,' said June's voice. 'I like the Lairds well enough but you can't really let your hair down with an employer, can you?' Honey thought that June was beginning to show a talent for enquiries. She also thought that there was a trace of mischievous amusement in June's voice. If the pair came to trading revelations, what secrets might June reveal?

'You're a gowk if you do,' said the older woman. 'But I could no more let my hair down with the Doctor than fly. I'm no more than a piece of furniture in that house with his "Do this" and "Do that". And Mr Samson's little better.'

'Mr Samson? He's the nephew, isn't he?'

'Yes. The Surgeon. They're a clever pair, I grant you, the Doctor and the Surgeon, very well thought of professionally but nobody could call them loveable. The Doctor acts very friendly with other men but there's never any real friendship. He asks a few of them to dinner from time to time and I've come to know his ways. Sometimes I think it's like a slice of toast with butter – smooth on the outside but hard and scratchy underneath. Mr Samson's the same.'

'There'll be no woman trouble, then? My two, they're still so lovey-dovey that nobody else could ever get a look in, always a kiss and a cuddle when they think my back's turned.' Things being as they were, Honey was not amused. She was sure that June was having to fight against the giggles, knowing perfectly well that the tape would be played and probably transcribed.

'Nothing like that.' Mrs Deakin sounded quite shocked. 'There's not been a woman over the threshold since Mrs McGordon left, not in that sort of way. Even when she was here, they did little more than share the house. And I'd have known if he had a fancy woman somewhere. A woman can be hidden but the laundry aye gives away any such carryings-on.'

The conversation was interrupted while June made tea and put out biscuits. Honey had time to consider what she was hearing. Mrs Deakin seemed remarkably perceptive and articulate, considering her background. Her observations on the Harrison-Hargreaves divorce would be worth hearing.

'Whatever did become of Mrs McGordon?' June asked. 'Do you ever hear from her?'

Mrs Deakin's derisive grunt came clearly from the tape. 'Not a word. The Doctor's had some letters from Canada but the envelopes were typed and he's not the sort to read out bits of news to the servants.'

Despite June's best efforts, the conversation drifted away into domestic matters. Shopping predominated and Mrs Deakin was indignant at being left to bring home by bus whatever she could not have delivered.

'The Lairds are quite good in that sort of

way,' June said. 'There's always one of them will bring a car to pick up the week's shopping at a weekend. Or, if not, I'm allowed to borrow her car.'

'The Doctor would never think of such a thing. Terribly fussy about his car, he is. Almost in tears when he got a wee dent in his front wing.'

Both Dodson and Honey sat up suddenly. The possibility of a hit-and-run was alive again. June was alive to the chance. 'Who did the repair?' she asked. 'Mrs Laird was far from pleased with the service she got after she put a dent in the Range Rover.'

'I did nothing of the sort,' Honey said aloud.

'Mr Samson took it to a man he knows in Aberdeen. Well, why not? It was Mr Samson himself that put the dent in the wing against the Doctor's gatepost. If the Doctor's had a dram too many he'll sometimes phone Mr Samson to come out by taxi and drive him home, but that time he was wishing he'd chanced it and driven himself.'

A few more minutes were wasted in discussion of the Doctor's drinking habits without revealing anything new. It seemed that the Doctor liked his dram but remained a gentleman and knew when to stop; but it was not unknown for him to chance the breathalyser when his nephew was not available.

'They must be really close if Mr Samson's prepared to turn out late in an evening to go and drive his uncle home,' June remarked. 'And I believe they go on holiday together?'

'Never,' Mrs Deakin said. Honey and Dodson had time to raise eyebrows at each other. 'The Doctor sometimes takes a week at a golfing hotel and Mr Samson goes off on his own with some tart.' Mrs Deakin's disapproving sniff came clearly off the tape.

'Somebody said that they went abroad together.'

'That's different.' Mrs Deakin sounded amused. 'That's work. Give their services for nothing, that's what they do. In Bosnia and such-like places. Well, I suppose they can afford it. A different place each time and usually they bring a patient back at their own expense, sometimes two, would you believe?'

'Yes, I think I would,' June said. 'There's a lot of doctors do that. Give their services free, I mean. I think it helps them with their taxes. I don't know how – it's all Greek to me. Do they book through a travel agent? Mrs Laird was looking for a good one. She was fizzing, last time they went abroad.

Their hotel reservation hadn't been confirmed, the town was full and when she phoned her travel agent they said they couldn't do anything about it.'

'My two always book through Hunter-Gourdon World Travel and they've never had any trouble.' (Honey and Dodson exchanged nods.) 'The time there was a strike and it looked like they'd get stuck in Athens, they cabled Hunter-Gourdon who soon sorted out another way home for them. They took the train into Switzerland and flew from there, but their patient had to wait and follow along later.'

The unreliability of service companies, and the fact that a firm is only as good as the person dealing with your order, took over the conversation despite brave efforts on June's part to drag in such topics as filing and shredding. When the tape ran out, June was called in from the kitchen and she was able to assure them that nothing else of value was said but that the two housekeepers had parted on the best of terms with promises to meet again soon.

'You did very well,' Honey assured her, 'and if anything comes out of it you'll get your holiday.' She waited until June had returned to the kitchen. 'As for you, Allan, you'd better go and use your charm on somebody at the travel agents. We want the dates and places of their foreign trips, to compare with the Doctor's bank statements. I don't know what that will tell us but it will surely tell us something. Then get yourself round to Meadowbank House. We want to know who, if anybody, has left the Doctor or his nephew money recently.'

Dodson began to look as though the world was going out of focus for him. 'How–?'

'How do you extract that sort of information? I don't know,' Honey said. 'Do something clever.' She was beginning to have faith in Dodson as an investigator. Perhaps she should marry him off to June. They could raise a whole new generation of detectives – possibly, she thought, in a house called Sherlock Home.

'What's the joke?' Dodson asked anxiously, wondering if he had done something silly.

Honey erased her smile in a hurry. If Dodson was so tuned to her nuances of expression, she would have to be careful about thinking such silly jokes. 'No joke,' she said. 'No joke at all.'

## Chapter Ten

She was already late for her coffee with Felicia Aston and Marjory Allen. In her youth, Honey had more than once landed in a pickle by missing a bus or train. That lesson learned the hard way, she had become a compulsively early arrival, sometimes being on the station platform half an hour before the train could possibly pull in. She had now achieved a sense of proportion and took a pride in turning up on precisely the due moment. She still hated above all things to be late for anything. It was now well known among the lower ranks that any meeting that Honey was to chair would begin on time and anyone arriving late would be amazed to read in the minutes what tasks they had volunteered for.

She looked around for June, who was not to be seen. So much for good resolutions. She tried to hurry out to her car but June erupted out of the toilet under the stairs. 'I'm not having you drive around in your condition,' she said. 'That's asking for trouble.'

Honey might well have objected to being ordered around by her housekeeper, but it was a good time for giving in gracefully. She filed the words away for later retaliation. 'The last thing I want to do is to drive,' Honey said. 'Sitting in a folded position brings my knees up and they get in the way of the bump and I end up getting indigestion. You drive me.' June began to turn away. Honey grabbed her arm. 'Like now. I have my car key.'

'I haven't got any knickers on.' They had the house to themselves but June whispered anyway.

'Nobody will know. Come quickly.' June was about to double back into the toilet but Honey had a grip on her wrist and pulled. Nothing infuriated Honey so much as being kept waiting while somebody else pottered about doing something that could well have waited, but her compulsion to be on time for appointments, itself an annoying habit when taken to extremes, was usually a redeeming virtue. June found herself, knickerless, in the driving seat of the Range Rover. She kept pulling her skirt down as she drove.

It was a gloomy afternoon, made gloomier by the approach of dusk. June had used the journey-time for a homily on being careful with her sacred burden. In Honey's view she was already according her sacred burden at least as much care as was reasonable and it was not the job of a housekeeper, even one who seemed destined to end her days as a faithful old retainer, to read her employer lectures on the subject. As they arrived at the door of the Starbucks, Honey was beginning to seethe.

'When the baby's born,' she said, 'I'll look to you to keep her safe, but while she's still weighing me down she's my responsibility.' Honey straightened up on the kerb, with some effort, and added loudly, 'Go home. Put your knickers on and keep them on this time. I'll get a taxi back.' She turned away quickly. Nobody had paid the least attention but June, who had been reared with great propriety, was very red about the ears and cheeks. Honey, on the other hand, felt better.

Inside the half-empty Starbucks, she was met by warmth and humidity. Felicia Aston was sitting with a lumpish, round-faced woman who was wearing one of the very long skirts so fashionable with the young and also welcomed by ladies with unlovely legs. Her hair was unnaturally dark. She could have passed for forty but her neck and hands betrayed a substantially greater age.

Honey took the vacant chair and was introduced to Marjory Allen. She asked the waitress for a glass of milk.

They chatted for a minute or two about the weather and Honey's pregnancy. Miss Allen, in keeping with her former employment, proved knowledgeable but rather old-fashioned.

'Honey Laird lives next door to Dr McGordon,' Felicia said suddenly. 'Miss Allen was his receptionist and almost everything else for years.'

'Ah yes. The Doctor,' Miss Allen said. A smile illuminated her pudding face. 'Such a gentleman!' Felicia Aston managed not to flinch.

It was obvious that Marjory Allen remained a hopeless worshipper at the Doctor's shrine. Honey took less than a second to make a total revision of her carefully planned approach. From the several accents that she had learned during a youth partly spent among aristocracy, she slid gently into the one that she considered to be the most likely to impress. 'I'm sure that you can keep a secret.' Miss Allen nodded, wide-eyed. 'As his neighbour, I was approached by the Palace. Dr McGordon's services to medicine, especially in the underdeveloped world, have been noticed. He has been recommended for an OBE, which might even lead on to higher things, perhaps even a K, and I've been asked to comment and make a recommendation. It looks as though it may go through on my nod, but if word leaks out it could put it back for years.'

'I won't say a word,' Miss Allen breathed. Her eyes were alight.

'That's good. And I must have the absolute truth. The other thing that could spoil his chances would be if it's discovered that somebody has been ... let's say, exaggerating.'

'Oh, but I understand. And I'd have no need to exaggerate,' Miss Allen said earnestly. 'Nobody ever deserved an honour more. The Doctor's such a *good* man. Not in a churchy sort of way but from within. You know what I mean?'

'I know exactly what you mean,' Honey said, although her interpretation might not have tallied with that of the older lady. 'But a question is bound to be asked about why his wife left him. Has there been a divorce?'

Miss Allen bridled. There may now be a generation that divorces as easily as it married, but the old prejudice against divorce still lives on among the elders. 'Certainly not, although the Doctor had grounds enough, her running off to Canada like that, and no doubt sex was at the back of it.' Miss Allen sniffed. 'She was always a flighty piece, making eyes at all the men. But the Doctor was aye the gentleman, keeping himself to himself. He should never have married that one. It was a relationship bound to end in tears.'

'Have you heard from Mrs McGordon since she left?'

'No. Well, I wouldn't expect to. She knew what I thought of her. A trollop.' Miss Allen rolled the word around her tongue with relish.

'And never any suspicion of a scandal concerning the Doctor?'

Miss Allen drew in her breath with a hiss. That the question was asked at all had shocked her. 'Nothing like that at all. After all, he's still a married man, however she may be behaving, and he never forgets it. When he examined a woman patient there was always a nurse present, or very often myself, and I can assure you that his manner was very professional. I still keep in touch with my old friends on the nursing staff and they say that he hasn't changed. After all, it's only been a few months since I...' Her voice tailed away. Evidently she had retired with

144

reluctance. Also, to retire was to admit to ageing. That word had not survived in her vocabulary.

In the face of so much devotion there would be no point in following up that line of country. Honey was beginning to suspect that the Doctor could have committed an indecent assault under Miss Allen's nose and it would have been written off as a display of playful affection. 'He seems to be very well thought of as a doctor,' Honey said.

'Oh, he is. Other doctors even refer patients to him if the diagnosis is difficult, and most patients trust him absolutely. Ladies sometimes dislike his bluff manner but the men swear by him as a doctor.'

Honey kept her tone light. 'None of the ladies ever developed a crush on him?'

'You might expect it, but no. Never!'

Felicia Aston had been sitting back in silence, seeming very much amused by the interplay. 'Oh, come on,' she said suddenly. 'You know that they either love him or hate him. Some of them drool over him. They probably have pictures of him pinned up over their beds.'

Miss Allen managed to combine expressions of pride and disapproval. 'If they do, the Doctor would never know about it, or approve if he did.'

'But none of them was ever grateful or devoted enough to leave him a little something in their wills?' Honey still kept her tone light, as if joking.

'I never heard of any such thing, but I certainly wouldn't be surprised. Most probably the person's still alive, in which case the Doctor himself wouldn't have heard about it either. He did so much good to so many people that some of them are bound to remember him, however ungrateful most turn out to be. Anyway, the people who had most cause to be grateful to him would never have had any money to leave. It's all very well that this country may give him an honour, but really if any country should give him an honour it would be somewhere like Brazil or Kosovo,' Miss Allen said indignantly. 'Flying around and taking Mr Samson with him and bringing patients back to this country, all at his own expense, treating the poor people for nothing. And doing the same in Edinburgh, only of course he doesn't have to fly anywhere.'

'Of course not.'

Having struck the equivalent of a gusher, Honey was reluctant to turn the tap off; but although Marjory Allen could undoubtedly have talked for hours on that subject she was offering few hard facts and only favourable opinions of the Doctor. It was time to divert the subject from mere eulogy and probe for something pointing in the direction of fact. 'Tell me about his opinions. Does he favour abortions?'

'Certainly not.' Miss Allen looked and sounded shocked. 'I've heard him say that a doctor's duty is to save life, not to terminate it. The only time that I ever heard him raise his voice in the consulting room was when some woman asked about an abortion for her teenage daughter. He feels the same about euthanasia. He lectured one of his partners in my hearing once. He said that allowing a terminally ill patient to slip away was one thing but to help them on their way was against the laws of man and morality.'

The Doctor's views, as quoted by Miss Allen, were gall and wormwood. If the reporting of them was inaccurate, Honey could see no way of proving it. She struggled to keep the mildly pleased expression on her face, reminding herself that proving the Doctor to be the very picture of innocence was still within her remit. 'That sounds very satisfactory,' she said. 'In your time, did he have any drug addicts among his patients?'

'Oh yes. They need doctors as much as anybody else or perhaps more.'

'He treated their addiction?'

'Yes. But strictly by the book. Decreasing doses of methadone and so on and so forth, plus the services of the therapist. I was responsible for keeping the keys of the drug store and the records of drugs purchased and used. I would have known immediately if the rules had been broken.'

Hope, which had begun to gleam in the darkness, flickered and died. Miss Allen's control of the drugs supply might seem conclusive except perhaps in the matter of euthanasia. Too many common or easily synthesised products were available for use, with little or no risk of detection, by any doctor prepared to sign the death certificate. Ten further minutes of carefully slanted questions took Honey no further. Miss Allen's devotion to the Doctor was so blind that in her view he could do no wrong. Honey could sense signs of malicious amusement emanating from Felicia Aston. She decided on one desperate last resort.

'This all sounds very satisfactory,' she said. 'But there have been one or two whispers reaching us that I'll have to track down and confirm or deny.'

Miss Allen froze like a startled rabbit. 'What sort of whispers?' she asked at last.

'Oh, I couldn't possibly tell you that,' Honey said. 'But can you suggest anyone who might be malicious enough to invent stories about him?'

She was prepared for a reply on the lines of 'everybody loves the Doctor', but to her surprise Miss Allen nodded. 'There have been one or two over the years,' she said sadly. 'Mostly people for whom the Doctor refused to do a favour. Addicts wanting an extra fix; somebody wanting a medical certificate that wasn't due them; others (mostly women, I'm sorry to say) who've convinced themselves that they have something serious and fashionable wrong with them and the Doctor wouldn't agree or help them to jump the queue for the scanner or for treatment. But I wouldn't know where any of them are now and anyway they've probably forgotten all about it.'

Felicia Aston stirred again. 'Wasn't there some sort of a quarrel between the Doctor and a male nurse?' she suggested.

'You mean Harry Kristmeier? There was certainly friction there,' Miss Allen said reluctantly. 'He headed the small nursing team but he also acted as practice manager. I believe he had some sort of degree in business management, or else he was still studying for it, something like that. A gipsyish sort of man. You could just imagine him having the morals of an alley cat, so of course he and the Doctor never got on. After he left, the duties were shared around. He was just the malicious sort who would bear a grudge.'

What sort of a grudge?' Honey asked quickly.

'I wouldn't know anything about that. I wasn't privy to their squabbles.'

'Did he leave Edinburgh?'

'That's something else I wouldn't know,' said Miss Allen. 'But I saw somebody in Jenner's last week who looked very like him.'

Honey dragged the conversation back to the overseas journeys but Miss Allen clearly knew no more than that such trips had taken place. In the end, Honey gave up. She thanked both ladies and was promised any further help that Miss Allen could possibly provide. She escaped into the dry cold of the street. She already had her mobile phone in her hand but a taxi was setting down a fare a few yards away. She just managed to get to it in front of a fat woman with two children.

As soon as the taxi had moved off, she wrote down the name. Harry Kristmeier.

## Chapter Eleven

When the taxi deposited Honey at her door, the motorcycle was parked outside and PC Dodson, already stripped of his leathers and enjoying a mug of tea with a clearly furious June, was lying in wait for her. He followed her into the study. Honey had no intention of being kept on her overloaded feet and dropped into the desk chair but Dodson seemed too upset to consider bodily comfort, and not only by having born the brunt of June's indignation. From his puzzlement, Honey gathered that June had been too coy to reveal the exact nature of the offence.

She had hoped that Dodson's presence would signify another forward step, but apparently this was too much to hope for. 'I went to Meadowbank House,' he said. 'But what you want would take a year, minimum. There's no sort of index and no kind of computerised record. If you know whose will you want to see, you can ask for it. Otherwise, put it out of your mind. There are researchers you can employ to do a search, but they cost the earth and take for ever, and I don't see the Super authorising that sort of expenditure or waiting that long, do you?'

'No, I don't. Now park yourself,' Honey said. 'Do sit down and stop looming over me, this room's too small for that. I'm sorry if I stuck you with an impossible task. I've suffered the same fate, so it's only fair that I get to spread the irritation. Here's the next one – or, to be honest, it's the same one but made a little bit easier by what I've just been finding out, so never say that I'm not good to you.'

Dodson took the other chair. 'I'd never say that about anyone who lets me wash their dog,' he said gloomily.

Honey was delighted to see that he had retained at least a vestige of his sense of humour, but she refrained from acknowledging the joke. 'Be my guest, any time. We know which travel agent the Doctor uses – the Hunter-Gourdon World Travel. See them and find out, discreetly, the dates of his trips to poorer countries. I'm sure you can sweet-talk some poor girl into looking through the files for you. Compare that with the bank statements. Cross off large sums deposited shortly after returning from one of those trips, we're assuming that they're something else altogether. Look for any other large deposits. Then go through the death certificates. Look up the wills of any patients who died before the date of that deposit.'

'How long before?'

'That's the puzzler, isn't it?' Honey brooded for some seconds. She had had little experience of executry, except in cases in which the proving of the will was seriously delayed by some suspicion as to the cause of death. 'The bigger the estate, the longer it takes. If lawyers are involved, my guess would be six months to a year. Anyway, fish around a bit and see what you can turn up. If you can find any large deposits following after a death certificate signed by the Doctor, and not associated with one of his foreign trips, look up the will.'

'I used to think that I'd fancy CID,' Dodson said. 'Now I don't think that I'd like it at all.'

'I can quite see that you might prefer to spend the rest of your police career breathalysing motorists, mopping up the blood after fatal accidents or breaking the bad news to the doting mothers of bikers. Personally,' Honey said, 'I prefer a vocation that lets me use my brain and doesn't put me in danger of physical assault quite so often. I was thinking of putting you forward for a transfer, but if you prefer it in Traffic, I shan't bother.'

'I'll let you know when we've solved this one,' Dodson said. But he was looking distinctly happier as he left.

Honey reached for the telephone directory. There was only one Kristmeier listed and the initial was H. That made it a virtual certainty that this was the Harry Kristmeier who had worked for, and fallen out with, Dr McGordon. Honey tried the number but got an 'unobtainable' signal. She tried again and received an 'engaged' tone. 'Third time lucky', she told herself and tried once more. This time she was told by a disinterested, recorded voice of a female Dalek that the number she had dialled had not been recognised.

Remaining determined that she would *not* call down a pox upon the heads and other parts of those who had buggered up the telephone service by streamlining it, she decided to try again later. Meantime she glanced at her watch and decided that she had time to look at any emails before her lunch would be due. There might even be something of interest. She set the computer to booting up, keyed in her service provider and told the computer to sign on. While it went through the motions she decided to check through Dodson's neatly word-processed reports.

A voice informed her that she had email. From the corner of her eye she saw the screen flicker. The panel had only one highlighted entry. Without allowing it to distract her, she clicked on 'Read' while continuing to do just that to Dodson's reporting, which was as neat and economical as the presentation of it.

The computer seemed to have taken a long time over accepting the email. She looked up, frowning. The message, from Canada, was short.

*The house at that address is occupied by two women. They are understood to be sisters. Neighbours advise that occupancy has not changed in at least the past year, possibly more. See attached photograph.*

A photograph would certainly explain the time taken for transmission of the email. She called up the attachment and looked again at Dodson's reports. He had been thorough. He would be an asset to CID; he did not have to like it although she could tell, despite his grumbles, that in fact he was enjoying himself – he just hadn't realised it yet. One success and he would be hooked.

The photograph was nearing completion. It was a good photograph, clear and sharp although it appeared to have been taken through the windscreen of a car. It showed two women walking along a tree-lined street. The trees were maples, the few leaves still hanging on were brilliantly scarlet. There was what could be a family resemblance between the two women, but neither of them resembled Mrs McGordon as Honey remembered her. She sent a message of grateful acknowledgement and set the printer to reproducing an enlarged copy while she tried the Kristmeier number again without any increased success.

She closed her eyes and put her head back while she considered the ramifications of what she had found out. An unsubstantiated accusation would provoke exactly the reaction that Superintendent Blackhouse was most anxious to avoid. Despite the mental turmoil, she began to doze. She snapped awake as June came in to say that her lunch was ready. Honey hurried to dab her face with cold water.

A single place was laid, as usual, in the dining room. June put a dish of thin but savoury-smelling soup in front of her and said sullenly, 'That was a terrible thing to tell the whole street.'

Honey, once the initial temptation to laugh had passed, was now overcome by compunction. She was beginning to regret the impulse that had tempted her into taking June down a peg or two. 'It was a simple tit-for-tat,' she retorted. 'You told Mrs Deakin that Mr Sandy and I were always kissing and cuddling when we thought your back was turned.'

A foretaste of a smile struggled with the sulks on June's round face. 'Well, it was true.'

'And it was just as true and just as misleading to say that you didn't have any knickers on. So there!' Honey said triumphantly. 'After lunch, I may want you to do an errand for me. I'll try the phone number again and if I still don't get an answer I want you to go to Leith Walk. See if you can get an answer from Mr Harry Kristmeier. If you catch him, ask him to contact me very urgently about a matter that he may find very interesting. In case you can't find him but he still lives there, I'll give you a letter to leave for him.'

'I'll go while you have your rest,' June said. Her tone made it clear that she was making a major concession and thereby heaping coals of fire. She removed the soup bowl and put down a plate of cold meat and salad. Honey would have preferred something hot and greasy with curry.

Lunch finished, she tried the number again and then ran off a letter to H Kristmeier. With the letter dispatched in the care of June, she composed herself on the couch for her afternoon rest. Suppose, she thought, that the Doctor had indeed disposed of his wife. In the statistics of known murderers, doctors had a significant place; but a doctor was so advantageously placed for successful and unrecognised murder that many times that number might be guilty. But how would a doctor dispose of a body? The preferred answer would be to let it be a body that had apparently died of natural causes. Why had Dr McGordon not chosen this route? Perhaps the fact that he had been known to have quarrelled with her had, in his opinion, made that method unsafe. What then?

Honey had been looking at the problem through the Doctor's eyes. Looking at it instead with the eyes of the undertaker she realised that, if invited to deal with a body that came complete with a proper death certificate, the undertaker would not enquire whether the house from which he was hired to transport the body was rented or the identity of the deceased real. If the other formalities, such as the funeral service and the grave, had been properly completed he would go ahead. Even the grave would be unnecessary in the event of a cremation, the ashes being delivered into the hands of the suitably downcast Doctor who had then no doubt allowed them to blow into the Forth. Dulcie McGordon might well be resting under a fictitious headstone in some large and impersonal graveyard on the further side of Edinburgh – Leith and Musselburgh sprang immediately to mind – or polluting the beaches around the Neuk of Fife.

Having thus drowsily resolved the entire mystery, Honey fell asleep. She seemed to fall asleep now at the drop of almost anything. She was doing everything else for two, why not sleeping? The sound of the front door, closing on June's return, woke her. She called out and June put her head round the door. 'He still lives there but the lady next door told me that he was at his work,' she said. 'There must be something about him, because I could almost see her knees shaking when she said his name. Anyway, I left the letter.'

'Thank you, June.'

'And you have an appointment with Dr

Gillespie at two-thirty. I'll drive you.'

'Ring up and cancel it.'

'That,' June said defiantly, 'I won't do. You're near your time and you'd be mad not to have your gynie check-up. My cousin didn't bother and she ended up having a breech birth behind the English goal at a rugby match at Murrayfield. So just you be ready in ten minutes or I'll phone Mr Sandy to come and deal with you.'

One glance at the other's face assured Honey that this was not the usual half-joking clash of wills. June meant it. What was worse was that June was right for once. She fetched her coat.

'Everything seems to be in order,' said the Doctor. 'There was nothing untoward in your last scan. She has all her fingers and toes and nothing that shouldn't be there. All the signs are for an easy birth and a perfect baby.'

'How long now?'

'You'd have to ask God or Mother Nature that one. Your baby's in position but the head isn't engaged. Not today and not more than a week. Two at the most. When the tummy-aches start I'll give you a closer estimate.' Dr Gillespie rather fancied herself as a down-to-earth, motherly, old-fashioned doctor jollying her patients along. Honey disliked the attitude but Dr Gillespie was a very good obstetrician so she stayed with her.

Honey had had to wait while the Doctor returned from attending a lady who had decided to begin a difficult birth considerably ahead of her time. Whether a birth should properly take precedence over a murder was, in Honey's mind, a moot point. Death, after all, was *a fait accompli* whereas it was still possible to do something about a birth. June brought her home in darkness and during the evening rush hour, to find PC Dodson waiting astride his motorbike and a message on the answerphone to say that Sandy would be late again and would eat out.

'I'm hungry,' Honey told Dodson, 'and I expect you're the same. Unless you have other plans, you may as well stay and eat with me and we'll bring each other up to date.'

Dodson only had time to nod before June said, 'Dinner in thirty minutes,' and vanished in the direction of the kitchen.

'I don't know how she does it,' Honey said, 'but if we don't sit down within thirty minutes, the food will be cold. I feel grubby. I'm going to have a shower and change. Enjoy the hospitality of the downstairs toilet and then watch the telly or something.'

When she came downstairs again, much refreshed, he was watching a *Forensic File* on Sky TV. They sat down within the thirty minutes. Honey noted with appreciation that June had done chops under the grill, small boiled potatoes, mixed vegetables from the freezer, and while the chops grilled and the potatoes boiled she had laid a perfect table. For that kind of service, Honey decided, she would put up with some impertinence.

'You still have to ride your motorbike,' she told Dodson, 'so I won't offer you spirits. I'm going to have a small glass of wine well watered, which is all that I'm allowed until the baby's weaned. In fact, I'm not even supposed to have that, but when I made it clear that I was not going to take dinner without at least a taste of a decent claret, I got that much of a concession. June measures it out and waters it. I could probably get more of a buzz out of a pot of jam that's gone past its sell-by date, but it wouldn't have the flavour. You can have the same or a can of a mild beer.'

Dodson chose beer. Honey sipped her diluted wine. She had rather gone off the taste of wine but had no intention of sacrificing it under pressure. When the first hunger pangs were satisfied she said, 'You may as well go first. How did you get on today?'

'Abysmally. If there's any kind of correlation between death certificates and deposits, I can't find it. Of course, it's possible that he's managed to confuse the issue, for instance by holding back a cheque for months before paying it in. Or he might have avoided cash altogether by recognising something valuable and saying, "If you really want to thank me, you could always leave me your Ming chamberpot," and then selling the gesunder for cash. Or he might have another account under a different name. But I can see all sorts of complications. He'd probably find it easier to cook up some really good explanations for the taxman. He couldn't really be worried that somebody might be looking for a connection, could he?'

Honey had finished her chop while he spoke. 'Probably not,' she said. 'Let the legacy question stick to the wall for now. If he's knocking off his patients, he may be doing it for the feeling of God-like power or out of a misguided belief in mercy killing. But we've no evidence of any such thing and I don't see any way to get such evidence without causing a ruckus.'

'If we come by one scrap of evidence...'

Dodson began.

'That would be different. A whole new ball game, as the gentlemen across the pond insist on saying. In that unlikely eventuality, I'll ask Mr Blackhouse to come out of the closet and insist on one or more exhumations. I'm sure he won't do it, but I'll ask anyway, in writing, just to put myself in the clear. What we do have is an email that came in today, from Canada, including a photograph of the two women who have been occupying the sister's house for at least a year. They're said to be sisters, which would fit. But neither of the women in the photograph bears much resemblance to the Mrs McGordon that I remember.'

'Wow!' Dodson was silent while June removed their plates, replacing them with dishes of hot apple tart and ice cream. When they were private again he said, 'Surely that's the evidence that you were wanting.'

'You think so? Think some more about it. We have an email from somebody I don't know enclosing a photograph of two unidentified women and suggesting that they've been the occupants of a certain house. We don't know for sure that Mrs McGordon ever went there, or she may have gone for a very short visit and moved on. It really needs somebody to go out to Canada, and I don't see a hope in hell, if you'll pardon my French, of that being authorised.'

'Then how do we check it out?'

Honey explained the reasoning that had been running through her mind that afternoon. 'I think that that's the direction in which a doctor's mind would work. Our first step is to go over the list of death certificates from the date when Dulcie McGordon left here. Then you check out the burials for those few months.'

Dodson produced a tatty and dog-eared printout from an inner pocket. 'There could be rather a lot,' he said doubtfully.

'Not as many as that,' said Honey. 'Cross off all the male ones – the undertaker would surely have noticed a sudden change of sex. And a death certificate records the age of the deceased, so you can cross off anybody outside the bracket thirty-five to sixty. And he wouldn't want a hearse calling next door just after telling everybody that his wife had run off. He could put her in a box or roll her in a carpet and move her himself. But he couldn't keep her around for longer than it would take to find a house or flat to rent and move the body. Start from the date of her departure and work forward for a few weeks. Look for anything unusual but, as I said, he couldn't have a funeral cortege leave from next door. Look at the addresses in the death certificates for houses or flats that were to rent furnished at the time. And no,' she added in answer to Dodson's look of bafflement, 'I don't know how. I can't think of any short cuts. You're the one with disreputable friends and a knack of wheedling information out of impressionable young women. Meanwhile, I'll see who I can find who really knew Mrs McGordon. More coffee?'

'Yes, please.' He held out his cup and sighed. 'I'll try the electoral register first.'

### Chapter Twelve

The next morning was cold and dry. The sky was clear and blue and the sparkle of frost, soon washed away by the sun, jewelled the plants in the Doctor's garden. It was a good-to-be-alive day. It was also Saturday.

One aspect of Honey's life had become a battle of wits. She was determined to live her life as fully as was compatible with giving her daughter a safe and healthy start in life. She thought that too many parents were prepared to abandon life in favour of their children; but if those children in turn repeated that attitude, who was ever going to live a life? June, on the other hand, was just as determined that the moment of birth should find mother and baby rested and ready to concentrate all their energies on facing the rigours of life and motherhood, respectively. It was, Honey thought, like the same scene viewed from opposite directions or seen in a mirror.

Sandy had hurried out to keep an appointment for a golf match, the semi-finals of a minor club tournament. Even detective chief inspectors, Honey insisted, need exercise and relaxation. It seemed to her that she and Sandy were arriving at a crazy situation in which each was overly concerned with the other's well-being even while their personal relationship seemed to be faltering; but while she was trying to keep Sandy active he was aiding June in trying to keep her passive. She would win in the end because her pregnancy would not last forever.

Instead of hurrying out of bed, or as nearly hurrying as her swollen physique would allow, Honey lay back on the pillows to spend an idle moment considering what came next in the case of Dr McGordon. Her mind was eager to turn away from the purely passive wait for nature to take its course. No doubt when she had a kicking, squalling, nappy-wetting baby in her arms she would find plenty to keep her interested and occupied. Meanwhile, however, she had one outlet for her energies, mental if not physical. She had quite forgotten to ask Dodson what his plans might be for the weekend, but he was unlikely to make much progress on a Saturday. He had probably decided to take an overdue day or two off. But what if he came up cold?

How else might a doctor dispose of a body? She really could not imagine a doctor, with a known face and a physique not accustomed to labour, carrying out a secret burial near his house. A doctor would be aware how frequently the results of such interments surfaced again. He would also know that advances in forensic science made it certain that carrying a body in his car would leave detectable and incriminating traces, but perhaps he was counting on the protection of a polythene shroud. The medical faculty of a university would have its own incinerator. A bribe to the chief technician, or to the staff at a crematorium, might work wonders, but at what risk! An acid bath seemed equally improbable. Did the Doctor have access to a boat for a burial at sea? June had not asked about any maritime connection. One – at least one – ingenious gentleman, she recalled, had hired one of the high-powered machines intended for reducing unwanted tree-branches to chips. He had passed a frozen corpse through it by night, directly into a river where the fish had done the rest of his work for him. Each of those options required transport. Had he hired a car or van? Thereabouts lay several avenues for Allan Dodson to explore. And next time that the Doctor's Daimler went in for servicing, could she possibly take dust samples for study by the forensic scientists? But that, she recalled, would result in an account for the cost being passed to Mr Blackhouse. The thought of his overblown face in that event was tempting but not quite tempting enough.

Or, of course, there could have been a fake accident. She must find out whether any female bodies remained unidentified.

She realised, quite suddenly, that she had brooded for too long. June had crept silently up the stairs and now bumped her way into the bedroom carrying breakfast on a tray. Honey was going to have breakfast in bed whether she wanted it or not. In fact, she never wanted it. The strain on her neck and back and the load on her coccyx were too great. But June's air of triumph, combined with pride more suited to a Labrador retrieving a shot pheasant, was too great to allow Honey to disappoint her. Honey thanked her fulsomely. June added that she would walk Pippa. Honey thanked her again, this time with more sincerity. June nodded graciously and withdrew.

Honey drank the orange juice, swallowed the cereal and began on the bacon and egg. She was too preoccupied even to wish that it had been grapefruit juice, porridge and a kipper. Of course, the fact that McGordon was a doctor did not mean that his sin had to be medical. Doctors had been known to commit assaults, to forge cheques, to rob, to ravish, to defraud, to be peeping Toms or molesters or to commit any of the other sins to which laymen were given. But surely Detective Superintendent Blackhouse could not expect an inspector in an advanced stage of pregnancy, aided by a single constable borrowed from Traffic, to investigate the Doctor secretly for every possible infringement of the penal code? No, if they cleared him of medical transgressions she would tell Mr Blackhouse that he would have to come into the open, assemble a proper team and investigate along established lines or forget it. And if she ended up as an ex-police housewife and mother, so be it. That had probably been her destiny all along.

Of course, none of the available crimes on her original list had been totally eliminated. Each had been shown to be unlikely; but they were still possible. Opinions could be mistaken. Informants could be wrong, deluding themselves or lying. She would have to go over the list again.

The coffee was cold, the last of the toast had gone soggy. She felt slightly nauseous but it soon passed. She put the tray, on its beanbag, aside and began the process of preparing for the day.

She arrived in the study while June was still out with Pippa. The house was silent. For company, she put on a CD of Antony Pay playing a Mozart clarinet concerto. Then, because it was too beautiful to keep to herself, she plugged in her headphones, detached one earpiece and tucked it into her waistband. The other earphone settled quite comfortably over her better ear and gave quite acceptable reproduction. She and her daughter could enjoy it together. The baby stopped kicking, which suggested that she was at least interested. Perhaps she would soon start to beat time with her little fists. Or even to conduct. Honey had been thinking of playing her set of Offenbach, but the thought of her unborn child attempting the Can Can was unacceptable.

Music, as she had discovered years earlier, made demands on an entirely different part of her brain than did logical thought. She listened with pleasure and half a mind while she used the computer in the preparation of a list of possible lines of enquiry. The music ran out when the first draft of the list was almost complete.

They never *had* exhausted the subject of smuggling. Had the Doctor – the two doctors, counting the Surgeon as a doctor – had they discovered a new method or subject for smuggling, something profitable enough to make the risk worthwhile? In the telephone directory under Turnhouse Airport she found Customs and Excise and she identified herself to the voice that answered her call. 'Tell me,' she said, 'do you usually look into doctors' medical bags or are they considered to be above suspicion?'

The voice chuckled. 'You have to be joking!' it said, in an accent that stemmed from not more than twenty miles out of Glasgow and in tones of tolerant amusement. 'We open anything that we find suspicious. Top of the list of things we find suspicious is whatever the public thinks we won't open. And top of *that* list is a doctor's medical bag. Does that answer your question?'

'It does indeed,' Honey said. She thanked her informant politely for dashing her hopes.

'One moment,' the voice said quickly. 'If you have reason to believe that a doctor is about to bring something in his medical bag–'

'I don't,' she said. She disconnected and began to brood.

She was roused from her reverie by sounds of the return of Pippa and June. Pippa made a boisterous entry to offer her mistress a morning greeting. There was a smell of the farmyard about her, but not bad enough to demand yet another bath. Honey sent her into the furthest corner of the room and told her to stay there.

June was still in the doorway. Honey thanked her again. 'When you see Mrs Deakin again,' Honey said, 'drag the conversation round to boats. Does the Doctor ever go out in somebody's boat? Does he have an inflatable boat in the garage?'

June promised to try. 'But,' she said, 'how

do I drag boats into the small talk? It's not the kind of subject we discuss.'

'Use your ingenuity. Does the Doctor like fishing or sailing? Or you could approach it by way of a man and his garage. We don't have a garage here, but if we did Mr Sandy would have it so full of things he'd otherwise have to throw away that we wouldn't be able to get even one car into it, let alone two. There would certainly be an inflatable boat. Does the Doctor clutter up his garage? Take it from there.'

June went away, muttering to herself.

The next item on Honey's list was to obtain a summary of serious unsolved crimes over the past few years. Being officially on pre-maternity leave, she could hardly trouble Records for it, and such wholesale use of the National Computer would certainly draw attention. She would have to ask Sandy to get a printout for her. She added a note on her computer, reminding herself to have Dodson check on hirings of wood-chipping machines. The next... She picked up the phone.

Felicia Aston's answerphone kicked in. Felicia might be at church (in which case, Honey thought, knowing Felicia's lifestyle, they would probably have to re-consecrate the place). More probably she and her husband had gone away, as they often did, for a weekend of golf and, it was readily admitted to their closer friends, wife-swapping. Honey left a message begging Felicia to call back at once.

She scanned her list again. She was deciding that a weekend of unremitting boredom was facing her when the telephone demanded her attention. PC Dodson was calling her. He thought that he might be making progress but he wanted to consult.

Honey's spirits lifted. Saturday might be a bad day for demanding information over the phone from official but non-emergency bodies but it was often a good day for catching people who had decided to stay at home and catch up with the week's chores. 'Do you have your bike with you?' she asked.

'Yes indeed, Mrs Laird.'

Honey glanced at her watch. She had risen late and time had flown while she was lost in thought. 'It's not far off lunchtime,' she said. 'I don't suppose you've made any arrangements. Come here and we'll find you something to eat.'

'Yes, Ma'am,' Dodson said with enthusiasm. Evidently he appreciated June's catering. Honey had gathered that he lived in digs, catered for by a landlady whose idea of cuisine stopped at the door of the takeaway. Sandy was not expected home for lunch but she warned June that there would be a guest in his place.

'That young Allan Dodson, I suppose,' June said with great disinterest.

Honey was always alert to nuances in June's voice, especially if they signalled a new romance that might eventually lead to a loss of her services. 'He has a girlfriend,' Honey said.

'Not now. She gave him the push.'

Honey's eyebrows went up. How did June know? 'And you have a boyfriend.'

'Nothing serious.'

'Well,' Honey said, 'don't you let him rush you off your feet. Allan's a real charmer but his bow has as many strings as a harp.' As she returned to the study she wondered if her last remark might not be taken as a challenge. Well, if their quest proved successful it would only be justice for Dodson to share June's reward of a holiday on Crete. The two could celebrate together. For a moment, Honey felt envy. A little dalliance under a Mediterranean sun would not have gone amiss.

To judge from the time elapsed, Dodson had had to come a distance, or else he had been caught up in football traffic. June allowed him a few minutes to get out of his leathers and make himself clean and tidy before she announced that lunch was ready. The only drink available was water. Honey noticed that Dodson was accorded the lion's share of the quiche. Even so, it was not a generous feed.

'You can fill up with biscuits and cheese,' she suggested. 'June has been reading articles about how important it is during pregnancy not to over- or under-eat, so whenever she thinks that she's been giving me too much I know that I'm in for a period of starvation and vice versa. At least mealtimes are seldom boring. Now, what've you got for me?'

'The website covering death certificates is back on line. Like you said, I looked out the details of certificates signed in the two months following Mrs McGordon going away.' Dodson had already finished his quiche and was applying blue cheese to an oatcake. 'Then I went to the central library and checked the electoral register. Some of the names and addresses weren't there, but that could have been because people had moved house. So I compared those with the phone books. Luckily they had Edinburgh directories going back several years. Anybody who had a phone listed for two years or more had to be real. That left me with two names.'

'Those names may have had unlisted numbers,' Honey pointed out. 'And not everyone has a landline phone listed in their own name. An elderly person may be living with a married daughter, for instance.'

'There's the rub. And it's no use looking for overhead telephone wires because most of them are underground nowadays and if somebody gives up the landline phone Telecom may not take down any overhead wires until the next time they're doing that sort of work in the area. I just couldn't think of an omnibus sort of question that wouldn't start anybody wondering.'

'I'm not sure that I can either,' said Honey. 'Presumably the two deceased were both female, so I couldn't pretend to be looking for the father of my child. I assume that you didn't think to go back to Meadowbank House and ask for copies of their wills?'

Dodson smacked his forehead, scattering oatcake crumbs. 'That would have told us whether they were real or not. I am an idiot.'

'You're assuming that they didn't die intestate. Don't be so hard on yourself,' Honey said. 'You're not an idiot. Just slightly dim.' (Dodson, who was gaining confidence, only smiled.) 'To be honest, I've only just thought of it myself and we're too late now, we'll have to wait until Monday. If you have anything you want to do for the rest of the weekend, now's your chance.'

'I've got my teeth into this and I don't want to let go now.'

'All right. But now stop and think. Doctor... Body... Disposal. Take the odds against having arrived at the right houses and multiply by the odds against having guessed the right method. To dispose of a body this way, he'd have to use a vehicle, probably his own car; but if he's going to take that risk he might as well drive to the west coast or to some lonely loch, weight her and sink her, or get access to an industrial incinerator. Despite the lapse of time, he still has the same car and the forensic scientists could probably give us a yea or nay. But we can't go within a mile of them. Fun, isn't it?'

Honey recalled a character that was said to leap onto his horse and gallop off in all directions. Allan Dodson, who had been showing similar signs of over-eagerness, slumped. 'You're right,' he said. 'We come up against all these queries which, in an ordinary case, I suppose you would usually answer by asking the right person the right question. But the people and questions we can ask are so limited that we might do better to consult a psychic.'

'I hadn't thought of a psychic,' Honey said. 'We'll add that at the bottom of the list. I do have one or two other lines to follow up, but my informant isn't available today. Well, I'm not very prodigal and I'm not a son, but I shall arise and go to my father and say, "Dad, tell me about frauds." Do you want to come as my driver?'

'Yes, of course I do,' Dodson said, visibly slipping back into hyperactive mode. 'Er – what do I do if you begin labour pains while we're on the road?'

'Unless you've done a first aid course in midwifery, you head for the nearest hospital in a hurry,' Honey said. 'Pretend you're chasing a motorist who parked on a yellow line or knocked over a traffic cone, or whatever gets your colleagues in Traffic to put the foot down.'

'Going home for lunch, usually,' said Dodson.

## Chapter Thirteen

June showed a sad lack of faith in Allan
Dodson's ability to drive safely while con-
veying such a precious burden. She had a
date to go next door for tea and cakes with
Mrs Deakin but she offered to break the date
and drive Honey wherever she wanted to go.
Allan Dodson showed signs of ruffled
feelings and Honey, knowing that a man will
tolerate almost any insult except to his viril-
ity or his driving, supposed that any prospect
of a romance in that quarter was definitely
over. Even when June was satisfied that
Honey had no intention of travelling on the
back of Allan Dodson's motorbike, June's
objections were by no means assuaged.
When Honey explained that Dodson would
drive her in the Range Rover June, who was
coming to regard the Range Rover as her
own personal transport, again questioned his
competence until Honey pointed out that he
was a qualified Traffic officer with all the
necessary tests and courses behind him.

Honey, while gathering up Pippa and the

dog's evening meal, explained to June, very firmly, that June's job was to remain at home, try to extract certain fragments of information from Mrs Deakin; and then to explain his wife's absence to Sandy, make sure that he took a hot bath after the chill of the golf course and provide him with a drink and a hot meal. June still had to be assured that Honey was warm enough and had her mobile phone with her and that Dodson was fully aware of the location of and preferred routes to the selected maternity home before she would move out of the way and allow the expedition to proceed.

'I don't remember my late mother making such a fuss when I was four years old,' Honey said as they pulled away.

Dodson was silent until they were halted at traffic lights. Then he said, 'You're lucky. I wish I had somebody to make that kind of fuss over me.' Honey nearly said that being fussed over was not all that it was cracked up to be. She would cheerfully have considered giving Allan Dodson one of her nursemaids. But no. When she came to think about it, June was indispensable. Sandy, on the other hand ... she did not know what to make of Sandy but he was essential to her life's happiness. She could put up with a little fussing.

Allan Dodson, as was to be expected, proved to be a more than competent driver. He filtered through the clutter of Sunday drivers without making a ripple or exceeding the speed limit, or even straying onto the bus lanes. Honey who, like most drivers, hated to be driven in her own car, soon relaxed and stopped treading on imaginary brakes. She discovered afresh that the passenger can see and enjoy much more of the view than the driver. Just as she made this discovery a morning cloud drifted aside and the gentle winter sun warmed the land and brought out the pale, harmonious colours of winter. With the trees bare of leaves, the distant prospects were more open to view. She took a deep breath and let an almost forgotten delight in the countryside of central Scotland take over.

She let Dodson choose his route and he took to the motorways. He took a chance on the remaining bottleneck before South Queensferry and was lucky with the eternal tailback. Then they were over the suspension bridge and back on the motorway. Dodson said that he had no preferences in music, just as long as it wasn't loud enough to distract him. Honey had a stack of discs in the back of the car, loaded into a rack that could deliver whatever was selected into the player.

She decided that she needed cheering up. They cruised to Perth through cold sunshine and to the sound of Gilbert and Sullivan operettas. Comic opera was a novelty to Dodson and he slowed slightly so as to hear every word. Gilbert's commentary on A Policeman's Lot had him nodding agreement. Honey began to direct the route, north and west from Perth. They were in surprisingly lush countryside, considering the season and the locale.

'What are we after here?' Dodson asked suddenly.

'Good question,' Honey said. 'Damned if I know. Perhaps it's a hangover from my childhood when I was quite sure that my dad knew everything. Anyway, I can trust his discretion and he's always a source of sound advice. Go left here. What's more, if he doesn't know the answer to a question he knows a man who does.'

'Now that,' said Dodson, 'is useful. And you're the person who knows a man who knows a man who does.'

'I hope so. Go right here.'

Dodson turned right and went back to his listening.

From a well-maintained B-road that undulated between woods and fields, they turned into a broad drive that ran between giant beeches, clumps of rhododendron and well-mown grass. The trees were bare so that they could see, between the rhododendrons, a comparatively small but undeniably stately home as it became ever closer. It revealed itself eventually as combining the best of Palladian style with the worst of Scottish baronial, yet managing to combine them in a manner that was dignified, charming and slightly humorous. Whether the humour had been deliberate or not had long been a matter for debate within the family. The gravel sweep supported some half-dozen cars ranging from a new Bentley to a rusting Mini. The house looked very well kept and, though it was a bad time of year for gaining a first impression of a garden, the lawns were clear of fallen leaves and tidily edged, the box hedges were well clipped and the coton-easter bushes were a blaze of berries.

'Well,' Dodson said, 'I'd heard that your Dad was well off, but I'd no idea.'

Honey was inclined to forget the impact that evidence of her father's wealth could have on visitors. 'I don't make a noise about it,' she said, 'and I'll be grateful if you play it down. Sandy and I don't let my father subsidise me by more than just a little. We prefer to make our own way in the world. I'll tell you something funny,' she added. 'When I finished at university, my father told me that he would stop my allowance unless I got a job. He nearly had a stroke when I joined the Met. He's got over it now and I think he's quite proud of me.'

'So I should think,' Dodson said stoutly.

'Thank you. Anyway, I don't want to be isolated from my colleagues, so don't go telling tales.' She touched the switch on the door. The window slid down, letting in a waft of cold air and a smell of winter countryside. 'Good afternoon, McMey,' she added to a figure, unmistakably that of a butler, that had hurried over the gravel.

'Good afternoon, Madam. They're shooting today.' He paused and listened to a faint popping in the distance. 'That seems to be coming from Hangar Wood. The next drive and the last will be Daunt Valley. I suggest that you join your father there. Will you be staying for dinner?'

'You'd better assume that we will. This is Allan Dodson, by the way. A colleague.'

McMey bowed. 'Mr Sandy was unable to come?'

'Mr Sandy had an important meeting on the golf course. He wasn't invited to shoot,

186

probably because I'd have been as jealous as hell. I daren't shoot until after the baby's born, not after the fright that we had.'

The butler smiled understandingly. 'Of course, Madam.'

'I'll see you later and you can give me all the scandal. Drive on, Dodson. Follow the drive round the house and then go left.'

Their way took them through a maze of farm roads. They passed a group of vehicles parked on a triangle of waste ground behind a barn. Their track dropped into a valley, crossed a broad stream by a hump-backed bridge and turned along beside the water. Dodson parked where Honey directed, on another small area of apparently waste ground. She seemed very particular about it. 'The other vehicles have to squeeze in here too,' she explained. 'And they can't go too far upstream or they'll be seriously in the way. You shoot, don't you? But not game or wildfowl.'

'How did you know that, Ma'am?'

Honey paused in the act of pulling on the boots that lived in the back of the Range Rover. 'I saw a cartridge box when you stowed your leathers in the panniers. The shot was small. Clay pigeons?'

'Yes. I've never shot anything live, except

rats. I've nothing against it except the cost. A friend tried to interest me in golf, but it seems a lot of walking for no return. After so much walking, I'd feel entitled to bring home something to eat, but I could never afford to shoot pheasants.'

'Not everybody can. Would you mind lacing up my boots? I have difficulty getting down so far. But clay pigeon shooting doesn't come cheap by the time you've paid for your entry and your cartridges. There are DIY syndicates, you know; the members share the work and take turnabout beating. Or you could try decoying for wood pigeon, or go to the foreshore after duck. Maybe you're perfectly content as you are, but nothing beats the thrill of eating meat that you gathered for yourself.'

Dodson looked up from tying Honey's laces. 'I know you're right,' he said. 'This stream produces trout, doesn't it? I fish when I can and I could see that most of the trees had been kept back from the bank, to give room for casting.'

'We'll make a detective of you yet.'

'You can't beat the flavour of a fish you caught yourself.'

They left the car and walked beside the stream. Honey leaned on Dodson's arm for security over the uneven ground. But their interlude of rural peace was ending. The sound of shots had died some minutes earlier. It was now replaced by the grind of vehicles. Two Range Rovers and a long-chassis Shogun came rocking along the track, followed by the Toyota pickup that always acted as game cart. They parked in line with Honey's car.

Mr Potterton-Phipps was the first to emerge from the leading vehicle. He was a tall man of around sixty, still lean and stringy but fit. His silver hair was thin but this was compensated for by a moustache of vaguely military shape. His tweed suit and boots had been of very good quality but were well worn. Honey's heart seemed to slip when she realised that he was looking older than when she had last seen him, but she kissed her father's cheek and told him that he looked well.

'Delighted to see you, my dear,' he said. 'To what do we owe?'

'I want to pick your brains. Sandy's golfing so I let Allan Dodson drive me through. I'm rather off driving while the bump gets in the way.'

'Your mother was the same. Good afternoon.' The two men shook hands. 'Always

189

happy to meet any of Honeypot's friends.'

'Don't use that name or I shan't come again,' Honey said; all the same, it gave her a moment of nostalgic pleasure to hear it used and on her home turf.

'Sorry, my dear. Keep forgetting that you're grown up now. I take it you're not shooting these days?' (Honey shook her head.) 'Does your friend shoot?'

'He does,' Honey said before Dodson could deny it.

'Good.' Mr Potterton-Phipps had a surprisingly youthful smile. 'This will be the last drive. Got to give the birds time to calm down and go up to roost. I've just had a message. There's a meeting going on in Montreal, rather an important one, and they want some figures in a hurry I'll have to go back to the house and fax them off. Allan can take my place. Use my gun, you're about my build. I was going to be at Number Three peg. It's quite informal. No loaders or anything like that. Honey will look after you. See you up at the house, my dear, and then I'll help you any way I can.'

He handed Allan Dodson a side-by-side shotgun, hung a heavy cartridge bag around the surprised young man's neck and slid into one of the vehicles. Within seconds he was battering one of the Range Rovers back over the bumps in the track.

Honey brought Pippa out of the back of the car. Pippa was too excited to dance; she panted and stuck to heel. This was her life and nothing else other than food held any real significance for her.

Dodson found his voice. 'For God's sake!' he said. 'Your father knows nothing about me.'

'He knows I'll look after you.'

Dodson was not sure whether he resented being nursemaided by a woman, but he recalled that Honey was his superior officer. He had developed such a respect for her that he would not have been surprised to find that she could heal the sick. He decided that her word would be law.

The underkeeper was in charge of the line of Guns. Honey explained the change of Guns to him, promised to oversee Allan Dodson and then introduced Dodson to his immediate neighbours. She explained that Peg Three was in a favoured gap where birds sometimes channelled through.

'I've never done this before,' he muttered.

'Well, you're doing it now,' she retorted softly. 'At least you don't have the sun in your eyes. Just remember that a side-by-side

191

may shoot lower for you than your own over-under. And pheasants are damn quick. Not as fast as clays, but pheasants look slow because they're big; then, when they're coming into range, you suddenly realise that they're going like rockets. Imagine that there's a clay pigeon just in front of their beaks, swing through from behind and shoot at that. Just remember that a bird that's going to pass nearer to somebody else is his bird unless you know that he's fired both barrels and missed it. And don't shoot at all unless you can see clear sky all round it.'

There was a pause while Allan Dodson assimilated Honey's words of advice. 'All right,' he said at last. 'But I'm not happy.'

'Happiness is not a prerequisite,' Honey told him. 'But you will be, I promise. The birds will be high, coming over the trees, but they'll look even higher. I'll try to warn you if something's really out of range. Now load and watch your front.'

They stood and waited. Pippa sat tight, quivering. In the distance could be heard, faintly, the tapping of sticks and occasional voices. Nothing else happened.

Dodson enjoyed stroking the fine walnut and feeling the perfect balance of the gun. He turned to look at Honey. 'Is it always as exciting as this?' he asked.

At that moment the first bird of the drive, a large hen pheasant, came with the wind behind it and downhill. It flicked over in silence and was gone. 'Not always,' Honey said. 'That was in range. Stay alert and focus your eyes on the distance.'

Birds began to flush, coming downhill at speed and the cocks blazing with colour against the dark blue sky. Dodson missed several, below and behind. Only reluctance to admit defeat to a superior officer whom he respected stopped him from handing her the gun and going back to the car. But Honey had the knack of seeing the shot string in the air, a grey shadow that flicked on its way and was gone. She told him where he was missing and, while he was still making up his mind, gave him instant advice as to whether or not the bird was safe, his and in range. He made the adjustment between clay pigeons and the larger, slower birds and he began to connect. He finished the drive with a spectacular left-and-right, high, fast and almost overhead.

The horn went. Honey was well known to the nearer picker-up, who more usually drove a tractor on the home farm. They exchanged signals and it was understood that Honey and Pippa would look after Dodson's birds. Pippa, in seventh heaven, did the job at a gallop and saw off a spaniel that tried to take over. The last bird was a runner and had to be hunted through deep cover. They saw the birds hung on the rack in the back of the game-cart pickup to cool. Honey judged that the bag was around a sensible hundred and fifty – not greedy but not to be despised. The beaters were emerging from the trees. Some of them had known Honey since she was old enough to join the beating line and there were greetings and enquiries. Pippa assumed that other drives were to follow and had to be put on a lead. Every line of her body language expressed disgust.

Most of the beaters set off on foot to return to their trailer. There was a gathering around the cars. The mood was sociable and one of fulfilment. Plastic glasses were used for drinks, which were served from a hamper in the back of the Shogun. Honey introduced Allan Dodson to the other guests. Most of the other Guns were accompanied by their ladies, who would have been conscripted, in most cases, for the drive home after the hospitality that followed the shoot. Some of the ladies had stood with the Guns, others had walked with the beaters. One lady had been shooting, very competently, while her husband walked. That couple had been unknown to Honey.

'You can have one beer,' Honey told Dodson. 'After that, you're on the wagon for as long as you're driving both of me. Did you enjoy it?'

Dodson sighed. 'Clay pigeons will never be quite the same again. And if I owned a gun of this quality I wouldn't let anyone else lay a finger on it.'

'Dad knew that I wouldn't let you dent it or scratch the stock.'

Mr Potterton-Phipps had still not brought back the other Range Rover. It seemed to be expected that Honey's car would make up the deficiency. The woman who had been shooting and her husband took occupation and a boy of about ten who had been among the beaters got into the tail with Pippa rather than be squeezed into the middle. The man had taken over their gun; he showed Honey that it was empty and then bagged it. They introduced themselves as Steven and Mary Fallow and their son Eric. One couple elected to walk. The others fitted themselves into the other vehicles. Heavily laden, the convoy travelled slowly back towards the house. Mr Fallow and

Eric, who had walked with the beating line, had been able to observe Dodson's final shots and were ragging Mrs Fallow, whose last shot had found only empty air.

The other Range Rover was waiting outside the front door. Honey's father came out to welcome his guests and to recover his Holland and Holland twelve-bore. Dodson had recovered the shotgun from Honey who had nursed it while he drove and he handed it over reluctantly. 'How did you get on?' Mr Potterton-Phipps asked Dodson.

'Six for sixteen,' Honey said.

'Not bad with a strange gun,' said Mr Potterton-Phipps. 'I've seen well established Guns go to pieces at that peg. We'll have to invite you again.' He looked at Honey. 'Remind me, next time you're coming. What did you want to discuss?'

'Can you spare a few minutes in private?' Honey asked.

Her father looked at his watch. 'Now is probably the best time. We have at least an hour before dinner and the staff is perfectly capable of serving drinks and directing people to the loos. Help yourself to drinks, carry them through to the study and I'll join you shortly.'

## Chapter Fourteen

The large entrance hall contained tables set with drinks and 'nibbles' sufficient to keep the guests contented until an acceptable time for an early dinner. Honey remembered the hall when it had been very dark and gloomy, but her father had caused the dark oak panelling to be painted cream and a new carpet patterned in buff and yellow laid, on a soft underlay, over tiles that had always reminded her of a public lavatory. Hideous Victorian stained-glass had been replaced by clear, and between the windows hung curtains of bright material which, added to the carpet, had the extra benefit of deadening the echoes that had previously reminded visitors of a church or the same public toilet. The overall result was the transformation of a gloomy cavern, well suited for setting a gothic film abounding in vampires and werewolves, into a bright and cheerful reception room.

Allan Dodson had been presentably dressed under his leathers. His motorcycling boots had been quite appropriate in the shooting field but would clearly have been out of place amid such fresh opulence. 'Shall I leave my boots outside?' he asked.

'If you like. Dad will probably appreciate the courtesy. I'll find you some slippers in a minute. And there's a cloakroom behind that door in the panelling. I'll feed Pippa and then I'll be back with you.'

He smiled his thanks. On his return, Honey met him with a pair of leather bedroom slippers. 'Property of one of my brothers,' she said. 'Do they fit?'

He slid his feet into them. 'They fit very well. Did your father really mean what he said about inviting me again?'

'I've never known him say anything that he didn't mean.'

'Wow! You didn't tell him that I'm only a PC. If he invites me again, should I accept?'

'You'll be bonkers if you don't. The sporting scene is a friendly one. Class doesn't matter and money is of only secondary importance.'

'Wow!' Dodson said again. A whole new horizon was opening up before him.

The guests were sampling the drinks and raising a babble of chatter. A young man in a black jacket whom Honey addressed as

Fergus served them with one beer and a watered wine. Honey led the way along a corridor panelled to match the hall and into the study. Here the resemblance ended. Only an elaborate cornice and the twelve-paned sash-and-case windows seemed out of place. Otherwise, the room was stereotypically the business office of a tycoon – very clean and uncluttered except for a fax machine, two telephones and the inevitable computer with its multipurpose printer. Even the customary bookcases had been omitted, their function presumably having been overtaken by the computer and the rack of floppy disks. The walls were relieved only by several clever ink and wash drawings that Allan Dodson remembered seeing featured in various art books and magazines but which he suspected were originals. The large desk confronted several upright chairs but the other half of the room held a group of easy chairs around a glass-topped table.

'While we're here,' she said, 'you'd better call me Honey and I'll call you Allan or people will start asking questions.' She smiled suddenly and disarmingly. 'Away from here, I'll tell you when you can start calling me Mrs Laird again.'

'I quite understand,' he said.

'Yes, I think you do. Let's make ourselves comfortable.'

Mr Potterton-Phipps joined them almost immediately. He was nursing what appeared to be a large whisky. He seated himself carefully, without spilling. 'That's better,' he sighed. 'I'm getting a bit long in the tooth for spending whole days afoot. How can I help you?'

'I'm not sure that you can,' Honey said, 'but you usually do. We're still looking into the matter of Dr McGordon and his nephew and we're still having to do it without making waves, so this remains confidential. We've sort of eliminated some of the more likely reasons why his conscience might be playing him up, which only leaves around ten thousand more. I'm going to ask Sandy to run me off a list of unsolved crimes over the last five years or so. But I thought you might be able to help.'

'If I can, I will. I've traced his investments, by the way. He's building up a nice little nest egg but there's no indication of where the money came from. Equally, there's no suggestion of insider trading. What can I tell you?'

'For instance, what are the preferred methods of fraud nowadays? We've eliminated the more obvious fiddle against the NHS.'

Her father settled himself more comfortably into one of the leather chairs and took a sip of his drink. From the scent, Honey identified one of the rarer malt whiskies. 'Presumably your doctor is above such humdrum matters as fraudulently claiming benefit. Most of the favourite frauds these days are by computer. Is the good doctor a computer whiz? Or a skilled hacker?'

'I'm pretty sure that he's not,' Honey said. 'Allan, remind me to get June to ask Mrs Deakin that question. That's the kind of roundabout route I'm driven to these days,' she explained to her father.

Her father nodded understandingly. 'If you discover that he has a talent in that direction, or that he has a close friend with that sort of skill, come back to me. He's hardly the type for credit card fraud. On a larger yet more mundane level, the preferred method is the Long Firm fraud.'

'What's that?' Honey and Dodson said together.

'If you want a fuller explanation, ask somebody in the Fraud Squad. In short, you establish credit with fake references, buy a lot of very expensive machinery on deferred payment, sell it quickly and vanish. Commonest, perhaps, in the building and allied industries and not suited to a doctor who is essentially established in one place and less able to disappear.' Mr Potterton-Phipps looked absently at the ceiling. 'There's been some selling of shares in a non-existent company, but they caught the culprit. Somebody is printing his own cheques, to use with stolen bankcards. I can't think of anything else current at the moment that meets the case. Of course, it has to be both big and successful before it comes to my notice. I'll pass the word round all the staff, including the lawyers, and I'll let you know if anything comes of it.'

'Thanks, Dad. I don't think anything you've said rings a bell, but we'll see. Now, what about smuggling. What are the favourite commodities?'

'Inward or out?'

Honey had never considered the possibility that the doctors might be smuggling in either or both directions. 'Either,' she said after a moment's thought. 'We know that drugs are the big deal but drugs don't seem to fit any of the parameters.'

'Very well.' Mr Potterton-Phipps frowned at the ceiling. 'Stolen goods, especially artworks, in either direction. They can't usually be re-sold in the country where they were stolen.'

'That's a thought,' said Dodson. 'Paintings from Italy, say, might well be smuggled as far as the Middle East and then travel under a patient on a stretcher. Please go on, Sir.'

'People, of course, usually inward and looking for jobs or National Assistance, but fugitives from justice outwards bound. Gemstones and semi-precious stones – Turkey is a clearing-house. And money for laundering. That's all I can think of for the moment.'

Honey knew that her father would not let the matter rest there. She would not be in the least surprised to hear from him again on the subject. 'And quite enough for us to be looking into for now. You've heard nothing against the Doctor since I last asked you about him?'

'Nothing. You'd do better asking Steven Fallow. He was a patient of McGordon's and he had a transplant done by that nephew of his or one of the nephew's cronies.'

'A kidney?'

'An eye.'

'I didn't know that they could transplant eyes,' Honey said.

'They can.' Mr Potterton-Phipps leaned

back and put the tips of his fingers together. Honey recognised the gesture. Her father was about to pass on some carefully edited words of wisdom that had reached him through one of his companies. 'I believe the difficulty is in getting a donor eye that's fresh, undamaged, the right size and a good match. The Gilberton Clinic has done several, I believe. I'm told that medical science is now so advanced that you can transplant almost anything that the donor can spare. An immediate transplant from a live and compatible donor has a good chance of success. The longer the ... the donation is separate, the worse the prospect. You don't really want to know all this, do you?'

'Dad,' Honey said, 'I don't know what I want to know, but if it's anything whatever to do with Dr McGordon I want to know it.'

'All right. Stop me if I get boring, but a company that I ... have an interest in has been doing some work in the area. There's been some research done into cold preservative solutions, cocktails carefully blended to suit the organ, but the main objective is to maintain ion balance and bind to the deadly oxygen radicals. There's been some talk about storing organs in PFC. The vital part of the trick is to keep it cold. Did you hear about the man who had a heart-valve replaced by a pig's valve? Quite common nowadays, I'm told. When they called him in for a check-up and listened to his chest, it was going thumpthump-thump-oink.'

Honey and Dodson had exchanged a meaningful look. 'Stay serious, Dad, please. So you wouldn't reckon that smuggling body parts would be practicable?'

'Almost impossible.'

'Is Mr Fallow pally with the Doctor?' Honey asked. 'I have to move carefully. You said that he was a patient of Dr Mc-Gordon's.'

Mr Potterton-Phipps looked at his daughter with one eyebrow raised. 'Wait here,' he said. 'I'll sound him out. I rather think that there's been some severing of relations. If I'm sure that he won't go running to the Doctor with the story, I'll send him through to you.' He rose, still nursing his drink, and left the room.

'This could be relevant, I suppose,' Honey said. 'The transplant industry. if you can call it that, is hedged around with restrictions. See if there's some blank paper on my father's desk.' She had a momentary vision of the Doctor murdering his wife in order to sell one of her eyes for a huge sum to a half-blind oil sheikh. Such acts had been committed in the past, though not usually among the more respectable citizens of Edinburgh.

The figure of Steven Fallow appeared in the doorway carrying a glass of sherry. 'I understand that you wanted a word with me,' he said. Dodson rose politely and Honey invited them both to be seated. Fallow was the sort of man who could disappear in a crowd; of average height, neither fat nor lean, with mousy hair slightly receding and no single feature that imprinted itself on the memory. The overall impression was of blandness and Honey, without knowing quite how she had arrived at it, had the impression of intelligence without strength of character. His eyes, she noticed, were dark brown. She recalled, while laughing at herself, that the description of Mrs McGordon had included blue eyes.

'I understand,' Honey said, 'that you are no particular friend of Dr McGordon?'

Steven Fallow frowned. 'That's true. But may I ask why that should concern you?'

'Did you know that I am a detective inspector with Lothian and Borders Police?'

'No. I didn't. Well, I do now. What do you want from me?'

'There is a matter concerning Dr McGordon,' Honey said, 'that needs to be investigated but without coming to the Doctor's attention. Confidentiality is paramount, particularly when a doctor is involved. Can I trust you to say nothing whatever to anybody?'

Few people can resist such an approach. For the first time, Steven Fallow's inexpressive face showed curiosity. 'I can very definitely hold my tongue,' he said firmly.

'That's good. Tell me about the Gilberton Clinic.'

'Is that all? I thought everybody knew all about it. I would have thought ... BUPA...'

'I've had membership of BUPA for most of my life,' Honey said. Her father insisted on maintaining her membership. 'But I've never had cause to take advantage of it until this pregnancy. If I cut my finger I go to my GP on the National Health and I've never had a serious illness. I've heard the name of the Gilberton Clinic being mentioned by people who've had operations and that's about the limit of my knowledge.'

Fallow shrugged. 'Every city has one or more of the type. They usually have better facilities and hygiene than NHS hospitals and the better NHS specialists and surgeons practise private medicine there. If you're rich or desperate, that's where you go.'

'And which were you?' Honey asked. 'Rich or desperate?'

'A bit of both. I wouldn't call myself rich, not while I'm standing beside your father,' Fallow said, smiling, 'but I'm tolerably well heeled. And desperate, yes. My left eye was never very good. Then I developed an abscess behind my right eye. They did what they could but eventually Dr McGordon warned me that the eye would have to come out. I'm a dealer in fine art and antiques, for God's sake. My eyesight is crucial to my living as well as my sport. Then McGordon said that he might be able to find a matching eye for transplanting. I said that I didn't know that they could transplant eyes.'

'That's what I said.'

'Well, we were both sadly ignorant. They can do it, but it's highly skilled work and to obtain the ideal one for transplanting is difficult because of the problem of fit – a kidney, after all, can be popped in almost anywhere – and because they deteriorate quickly once they're removed and also because nobody living wants to part with a perfectly sound eye, so it's expensive and unusual.'

Mr Fallow hesitated for some seconds. 'I paid the clinic a large, flat fee for the operation, the nursing and all the attendance.

There was no separate mention of the eye and I had to assume that it had come from somebody who had died. Was there anything wrong in that? Was I being naïve?'

'Perhaps,' Honey said. 'But if the facts are as you've just said, I don't see that you've committed any crime.'

Mr Fallow had tensed but now they could see him relax. 'That's all right, then. The way I looked at it, if somebody had a matching eye they were unlikely to be a friend or relative of mine. I was surprised when Dr McGordon said that it could be arranged, because I know that it's illegal in this country to buy or sell organs, but I had a vested interest in not asking any awkward questions.'

'But you went ahead,' Honey said. 'Did you ever know where the donor eye came from?'

Fallow shook his head and held up his hands in a negative gesture. Honey had the impression that if he had been standing up he would have backed away. 'Good God, no! Never. And I didn't want to know. I could picture looking out of my new eye and wondering what had been the last sight that the eye had seen before the accident or whatever killed its previous ... what would one say? Owner? Wearer? User?' He laughed uncomfortably. 'Anyway, I very much wanted not to think about where it came from. And I still do.'

'I suppose I can understand that. Who did the implantation? Not Mr Samson?'

'Mr Samson's a general physician. Mr Shezad did the operation. They brought him up from Leeds, I believe. Mr Samson only does innards. I believe he's *the* man on kidney transplants. They're much commoner, of course. We each have two kidneys but one would have been enough, so any near relative could, at a pinch, spare one. Eyes are different.'

'And when did your operation take place?'

'About two years ago. January the thirtieth.'

Honey looked closely. The two eyes matched and moved in unison. If there was a colour difference it was no more than can be seen in many people. Perhaps the right one was now artificial? Fallow seemed quite unperturbed. Evidently close scrutiny had become an everyday part of his life. 'And the transplanted eye is still in place?' Honey asked.

'Yes.'

Honey glanced at Dodson. He seemed to be getting it all down in shorthand. 'The operation seems to have been successful,' she said. 'The two eyes match well and move in unison. What did you fall out with the Doctor over?'

Steven Fallow's face remained expressionless but Honey noticed that his hands stiffened momentarily as though about to turn into fists. 'When I first came out of the anaesthetic, it seemed miraculous. I had laser treatment to the other eye, which improved it. But I found that I had slight double vision. I was told that it would get better but it continued to get worse. It hampered me in my business and it ruined my shooting and my golf. I was given exercises and now I can bring the two images together, but it takes a conscious effort to hold them like that. Well, when you need your vision most is just when you can't spare the concentration for holding two images together. I went back to McGordon. By then Mr Shezad had made his pile and gone back to lord it in Egypt or wherever he came from. McGordon said that he could refer me to somebody else who could correct the defect; but he quoted me a price that exceeded that of the original operation – which, God knows, would have been enough to buy quite a decent yacht. I have BUPA but they weren't going to look at it.

Eventually, I went to a different doctor and I'm going down to London for a remedial operation in March. And now, it's my turn to ask you to keep this confidential, because I had word through a friend of the Doctor that if I make any kind of a fuss he'll sue me and he'll warn the other surgeon not to touch my case.'

'Believe me,' Honey said, 'we've no intention of getting you in Dutch with any practising doctor.'

The fax machine began to type. Fallow looked at Honey sharply while he turned her statement over and over in his mind. Eventually he arrived at an interpretation that satisfied him. He furnished his address, phone number and email address, in case of further enquiries, without demur. He seemed to be on the point of asking a question of his own, which Honey guessed would be as to why they wanted to know so much about his operation. She was saved from the need to formulate a reply that would sound like an answer, but without giving anything away, by the return of Mr Potterton-Phipps. Honey remembered that, wherever he was in the house, the arrival of a fax would alert him by way of a series of tiny blinking lights.

'Food's on the tables,' he said. 'Only a buffet, but I think you'll enjoy it. If you've finished your talk, you'd better come through.'

Before they were quite out of the door, he was removing the fax from the machine.

As soon as they had eaten and had let Pippa out for a comfort break, they got back on the road. 'Quite an interesting day,' Honey said.

'Definitely. That beautiful gun that your father lent me has fired my acquisitive instincts. And I hadn't realised how sociable an occasion it could be. Clay-busting is much more competitive. I made no secret of the fact that I'm a humble copper but everyone was still friendly. They just wanted to know what I did and how I did it and whom with. I don't think that I gave anything away about our present case. After that, they just spoke about the shooting.'

'I wasn't thinking about the shooting.'

'I wasn't thinking about the McGordon case.'

'Nor was I,' Honey said thoughtfully. She had managed to get her father aside during the meal for a very personal consultation.

## Chapter Fifteen

Honey had contrived to keep her father away from the buffet table and out of his study for a quick and very private consultation. Mr Potterton-Phipps had been careful to hide his embarrassment. The subject was a sensitive one and his daughter was clearly worried. Following the death of her mother some years earlier he had tried to be both father and mother to her rather than go to the unnecessary extreme of marrying again, but despite the assistance of several ladies who would have been delighted to share the obligation he had found the burden wearing. It is no easy task for a man, however knowledgeable, to explain the workings of her body and mind, and those of a man, to a maturing girl. He had hoped and believed that that particular duty was in the past, but he found that a burden once assumed is not easily laid down again.

He listened patiently to a story that is as old as sex itself. 'I've no doubt you're right,' he said at the end. 'The approach of family can be a binding agent, but pregnancy can be almost as hard on the man as on the woman. If you've found sex uncomfortable, which is often the case, that's nature's way of telling you not to do it. You certainly shouldn't proceed with anything that hurts you. But Sandy may find the lack of it just as discommoding. In addition, unless you explained yourself with care and tact, he may very well feel rejected; in which case he may feel shy about risking further rejection by trying to heal the breach. This may well explain an apparent dwindling of affection on his part. You haven't been married long enough for friendship to take over from lust.'

'All very well,' Honey said, 'but what do I do about it?'

Mr Potterton-Phipps flinched. His staff would have been amazed to see their unvaryingly positive chief at an apparent loss. This was not usually a subject discussed between father and daughter. He called up his reserves, banished embarrassment and plunged ahead. 'The two of you have to figure out between you what works for you both. There are plenty of ways for both of you to achieve release without causing pain.' Pretending to meet her eye in an expression of understanding and compassion, he was in reality studying a minute freckle on her forehead. He went on to enumerate at some length more than a dozen alternative means by which frustration might be relieved. 'That's putting it bluntly,' he added, 'but, if I read you rightly, you were asking me to do just that.'

'Not that damn bluntly,' Honey said, 'but thank you anyway.' In his relief, her father was still chuckling as he watched their lights fade away down the drive.

Honey considered herself to be a thoroughly modern and emancipated woman. She had, she considered, 'been around the block' before she met Sandy. But, although her father had tried to convey his more detailed advice in a gentle and even oblique manner, she had been perturbed to realise how insensitive she had been in failing to guess at Sandy's needs. Her father's suggestions as to how to remedy the situation came as a surprise only in the context of herself and Sandy. She now had to pass the hurdle of introducing the topic with Sandy. She had been pensive on the long road home. By the time that Dodson had seen her safely indoors and left on his motorcycle, she had decided to take a firm grip on herself, face up to embarrassment and make the opening moves.

Sandy, for his part, had been both surprised and gratified to be called upstairs, to find the love of his life attired in her slinkiest peignoir (which, for the moment, would no longer quite meet at the front). She was armed with one or two marital aids, including some lubricant jelly and a pair of handcuffs. Any embarrassment was both hidden and unnecessary. Her mood was the mood of loving persuasion for which he had been longing. If the events that followed lacked the usual depth and lubricity in the culmination, at least the event as a whole, as well as being more protracted, was filled with the old delight.

Next morning, the two Lairds slept later than was usual even for an off-duty Sunday. When they rose, each was in a languorous mood. It was, she thought, as good as of old or even slightly better. They wasted a few minutes in neck-nuzzling before Honey said, 'You could do something for me.'

'Anything,' said her husband.

'I'll hold you to that, some time. But what I want now is a printout showing every major unsolved crime for the last five years.'

Sandy withdrew his face from her shoulder, yawned and frowned into hers from a range of only a few centimetres. 'You probably couldn't lift it. What I had in mind was something more like this.' His head vanished under the duvet.

Honey chuckled but got a grip on his ears. 'Come out of there, you idiot, or I'll scream for June. I'm looking for ideas, but not that sort. Of course, whatever Dr McGordon did may still be an undiscovered crime. But that's my problem, not yours. I don't suppose you can do anything to help until tomorrow. Go and play golf.'

'You mean that?'

'I think so. If you still have the energy. You made the date so you'd better go. I want to think, but with you in the mood you're in my thoughts would get stuck in a rut.'

'There's no polite answer to that.'

They ate a leisurely breakfast together before getting dressed. Sandy disappeared towards the golf course. Honey, while promising herself a leisurely day, opened her emails. Among a clutter of social messages and such minor advertising as had slipped through the net was one from Detective Superintendent Blackhouse:

*There is to be a meeting with the ACC (Crime), Tuesday, 11 a.m. in his office. Please attend, bringing with you such evidence as you have collected in the matter of Dr Duncan McGordon.*

*J Blackhouse, Det Sup.*

The afterglow of her episode with Sandy and the relief of having resolved the tension between them faded only slowly. In their place she became aware of extreme discomfort in the area where, she imagined, Dr McGordon's nephew would have pursued his speciality. If J Blackhouse Det Sup had sought the meeting, he would have worded it differently. It sounded as though the Assistant Chief Constable (Crime) was on the warpath, Mr Blackhouse was on the carpet and she was ... where? It seemed that somebody had whispered in the ear of somebody who had passed the word onward towards Dr McGordon. Just who the whisperer might be was irrelevant. The story might well have been passed on 'in strict confidence'. But if the identity of the whisperer should happen to come to her attention, no doubt Allan Dodson would be happy to provide an endless series of parking and speeding tickets.

The discomfort in her mid-section recurred. Did she have indigestion or was she developing an ulcer? She had no love for Mr Blackhouse. Earlier, she would have said that she would be only too pleased to see him go down the pan. Now, she was surprised to find that a sort of loyalty prevailed. She might not like him but she had got used to him. If his head rolled, whoever succeeded in his stead might not accept his view of her as an eccentric but beautiful genius but might instead see her as Honey sometimes saw herself, as a flighty and undisciplined hoyden. Or he might even regard her as fair game. Furthermore, she felt herself to be vulnerable. She had been the most active participant in the forbidden enquiries; and while she might be able to excuse herself at Mr Blackhouse's expense she might thereafter carry the stigma of disloyalty or even whistle blowing. And, the next day being Sunday, she was going to be very much hampered in doing anything about it that day. Retirement on grounds of motherhood seemed to be looming.

She leaned back in her chair and breathed deeply, telling her muscles to relax. She had never phoned Mr Blackhouse at home and she had to look up the number, but when she called it his telephone rang repeatedly without an answer.

Just when her deliberations were at their gloomiest, the phone rang. Kate Ingliston, apparently returned from her weekend jollity, was returning her call. Honey's first impulse was to put her off. But it came back to her that her original call had been made because there was one faintly possible line of enquiry open. It was a long shot. It was much more likely that Mrs McGordon had moved on and her place had been taken by another friend or relation or even that the police photographer had been misled into photographing Mrs McGordon's sister walking with some other acquaintance. It was nevertheless worth pursuing. It could not possibly be pursued to any sort of conclusion on a Sunday morning but perhaps Monday would allow time for an exchange of emails with Canada in preparation for the next day's meeting. If she could show that any avenue was open it might help to deflect the blow. She issued an immediate invitation to coffee.

Kate was on the doorstep within ten minutes, giving Honey time to enlarge a photograph on the computer before settling in the sitting room. Kate, now the butterfly still dressed and made up for her weekend of dalliance, was hardly recognisable as the caterpillar of the rest of the week. But while Honey was anxious to discuss the photograph, Kate was determined to explain over the coffee-cups why she had returned home

221

rather earlier than usual. It seemed that while Phil had enjoyed his liaison with the other lady (and rather too much for Kate's peace of mind) the gentleman had proved to be a disappointment. 'My nephew Simon,' she said bitterly, 'is better hung. And he's only six.'

Honey commiserated. When she could at last grab Kate's attention, she produced the photograph emailed from Canada. 'Do you recognise anybody in this picture?' she asked. 'I got the Mounties to send me a photograph of whoever the woman is who's living with Mrs McGordon's sister. To be honest, in the photograph I'm not even absolutely sure which is which. If somebody from around here was sent out there, or offered a home, in order to give the impression that Mrs McGordon was still alive...'

Kate was hardly listening. She studied the photograph. 'She's put some weight on,' she said. Honey felt hope rising. 'And she's bleached her hair and stopped bothering so much with her makeup, so she looks about ten years older, but it's her all right. This is Dulcie McGordon.'

Hope did a belly flop. 'You're sure?'

'It took me a few seconds, but I'm sure. Of course, you only saw her in the distance and not over a very long period; but I knew her quite well. Looking past those superficial changes, yes, I'm absolutely sure. You can't mistake the bone structure of the face. And she was slightly knock-kneed. You can see it quite clearly in the photograph.'

Honey fell silent. Looking again at the photograph, she could see that Kate was absolutely right. While Kate prattled on about the physical deficiencies of her week-end partner, Honey sat, sipping her coffee and numbly regretting what had been a very hopeful line of enquiry. Hope was going down for the third time.

The phone rang as she returned from seeing Kate to the door. Honey picked it up. As usual she only gave her number, which any caller must already know.

'Who am I speaking to?' asked the caller. The voice was male, deep, well modulated but with an accent that had not quite managed to escape from its origins somewhere in the Scottish Central Belt.

'This is Detective Inspector Laird. Who's calling?'

The introduction was usually enough to frighten off any random caller, but not this one. 'This is Henry Kristmeier.' Honey's recall was not usually slow but on this occasion it hung fire. 'You left a note for me,' the voice said impatiently.

Hope surfaced and began to swim for the shore. 'I'm delighted to hear from you, Mr Kristmeier,' she said. 'I have some questions to ask you concerning Dr McGordon. Could you possibly come and see me at my home?' June was busily preparing meals to last for the rest of the day so that she could take the afternoon off and go visiting. Honey had told Allan Dodson that he was free for the day or that if he cared to turn up they might be able to go a little further towards unravelling the tangled skeins of the case; but there had so far been no sign of him. With Sandy away from home she must face the discomfort of driving herself or call a taxi. A glance out of the study window showed that the forecast rain had arrived at last. 'I don't find travelling very convenient at the moment,' she said. 'Let's just say that my doctor discourages it.'

Mr Kristmeier considered in silence. 'How would I know that you are a genuine police inspector?' he asked.

'A sensible question. I can show you my identification. You can check my phone number with Lothian and Borders if you like. They won't give out a private number but if you quote this number to them and ask if it's correct for Detective Inspector Laird, they'll confirm or deny it.'

A smile came into his voice. 'I don't think that we need bother. I'll come to you. What's the address?'

Honey was busy with her thoughts about Dr McGordon, considering what questions she should put to Mr Kristmeier and what answers to hope for. In the light of Mr Blackhouse's email, it was surely rash to continue investigating and yet there was no other avenue of escape and, with care, there should be no leakage of the fact back to the ACC(Crime). Her deliberations were interrupted when the front doorbell rang. Only the vaguest shapes could ever be made out through the wired and obscured glass of the front door so she stooped to the fish-eye lens. She could see an elbow and a shoulder and, beyond, a motorcycle propped on its stand. Expecting Allan Dodson, she opened the door.

Where the man on the doorstep resembled Allan Dodson, the resemblance was exaggerated almost to the point of caricature. Dodson was tall but this man was taller. Allan was slim but the newcomer had an athletic leanness. Allan was nice-looking but this man was handsome and aware of it, with high cheekbones and features modelled in the best traditions of strength and masculinity. Where Allan was attractive to girls this man would, Honey thought, be sexually irresistible to women ... to most women, she corrected herself. He was the very stereotype of a stud, a sex god, and as an actor he would inevitably have been cast as such. He could have had a future in hardcore movies. It was lucky that she had made up her differences with Sandy last night, she decided, because while Allan Dodson might make a young woman's heart beat faster, this one could cause palpitations in quite a different place. While, at her invitation, he removed his wet leathers in the hall, he seemed to be releasing a cloud of testosterone, endorphins, pheromones, MHCs ... she ran out of names of male sexual messengers. And while she was noticing him, she was aware that he had taken in her pregnancy and found that it did nothing to detract from her own female magic.

Sternly telling herself that her knees were as firm as ever, she led him through and they took seats in the study. 'Before we begin,' she said, 'I'd like to know how strong is your loyalty to Dr McGordon.'

He locked eyes with her. All sexual signals seemed suddenly to be switched off. 'I don't owe him any loyalty,' he said. 'You tell me if your interest in him is because you want him painted in pretty colours so that you can use him as a witness, or are you after his blood?'

They could have fenced all day but she decided to be frank without encouraging him to fabricate slanders against the Doctor. It was too late for discretion. 'All that we're really after is the truth,' she said. 'But we have reason to believe that the Doctor has something serious on his conscience. If so, we want to dig it out.'

'I doubt if he has much of a conscience,' Kristmeier said. Given his appearance and his name, Honey might have expected a variety of accents, but an accent, which had been exaggerated by the phone, carefully suppressed but redolent of the Lothians, was somehow out of key. 'If you find that he does have something hanging over him, then what?'

'Then as far as I'm concerned the axe can fall.'

'But will it?' He leaned towards her. She leaned back rather than be overpowered by a surfeit of pheromones. 'I've had my suspicions,' Kristmeier said. 'I had a word with a friend of mine in the police, a sergeant, and she spoke to somebody else and the word that came back was that the Doctor had some powerful friends, some of them his patients, and that I might not be doing myself any favours if I took it any further.' He sat back in his chair.

Honey felt her blood pressure return to normal. 'That is why I have been told to do this from home. But your own personal view of the man?'

'So Dr McGordon is not flavour of the month with everybody in the police.' Kristmeier frowned. He crossed his knees and even managed to invest that simple movement with an air of masculinity. 'I think he's a crook and a charlatan.'

'Do you have anything to go on?' Honey asked.

'Judge for yourself. So that you'll understand, I'd better explain myself. I trained as a male nurse, but I couldn't see it as a lifelong career. Blood and urine and heavy lifting, spending every day surrounded by people who feel sorry for themselves. I'm not unsympathetic but a dead-end job among the sick and lame was not my ultimate ambition. I thought of studying medicine, but that would only be to climb higher up the same old ladder.

'I decided that the place to be is in management. I knew I was a good administrator but whether I'd ever be more than that I had to find out. I was taking a business degree course while working for Dr McGordon's practice, so I acted as practice manager as well as giving injections and sticking plasters on boils. Even then, I had my concerns. If I discussed them with colleagues and with others it was in the hope that somebody would put my fears to rest. It must have got back to him that I'd been talking out of school, because he called me into his consulting room. Fired me without a reference for stabbing him in the back, so he said.' Kristmeier's proud nose wrinkled in disgust. 'He had the wrong end of the stick. I could have explained but he wouldn't listen. And he still owes me my last month's pay. When I argued with him, he said that I could sue and the publicity would prevent any employer ever taking me on.' Kristmeier smiled grimly, which only added to his air of self-assurance. 'Well, I can do without him. I'm assistant manager of a small pharmaceutical supplies company now and when the manager retires in three years I've been promised the job. When that time comes, I'll be just as happy if a hostile and influential doctor isn't still in practice and spreading poison about me. But that's over and above the fact that I think he's a pig-turd.'

It was only as the thudding of her heart calmed and the tight band around her head relaxed that Honey realised how tense she had been. But now, a great change had come over the case. The team so far had comprised one pregnant inspector, a constable borrowed from Traffic and sundry ladies with patchy knowledge of the two medical men. Suddenly the hour had produced the man. Kristmeier – she almost laughed aloud – was just what the doctor ordered. He must have a deeper knowledge of the Doctor and his nephew than anybody else and he was deeply disaffected. If anybody could show her the Doctor's Achilles heel, this was the man.

'Before we go any further,' she said, 'and for the reason you've already touched on, this has to be in absolute confidence until we can be sure that we know where we're going.'

'That,' Kristmeier said, 'is pretty much what I was going to say to you. I can keep a confidence and I'm sure that you can.'

The questions were becoming clear in Honey's mind, but she was distracted by the ringing of the doorbell. There was no sound of June, so presumably she had already left the house. Honey got up and went to the front door.

## *Chapter Sixteen*

Honey jerked open the front door, determined to give the visitor a flea in his or her ear. She was not prepared to tolerate any interruption of what Kristmeier was, she hoped, about to reveal. But she suffered an instant mood swing. There were now two motorcycles on the brick paving, and so similar that for a moment she blinked in case she was seeing double.

'Come in,' she said. 'I'm glad you're here.'

'If you're becoming a biker, Inspector,' said Dodson, 'we'll have to found our own chapter of the Hell's Angels.'

'Come in, Allan,' Honey repeated, 'and cut out the nonsense. We have a busy time ahead. Get rid of your leathers and fetch another chair from the kitchen. I have Mr

231

Kristmeier here.'

'Oho! I was going to talk about yesterday with you, but for this I can wait.'

'If I still have a job in three days time, I'll take you out and show you how to decoy pigeon. For now, we're detectives.'

While Dodson fetched a chair, Honey called up Mr Blackhouse's email. Honey introduced the men. There were faint but immediate signs of hostility, the usual reaction of two men, each blessed after his own fashion with sex appeal, in the presence of an attractive woman. Honey, who was hardly unaware of her own attractiveness, took the familiar vibrations as normal. She turned the monitor so that Dodson could read it.

'Now Mr Kristmeier,' Honey said. 'Tell us as much as you can about the foreign trips that Dr McGordon and Mr Samson have been making.'

Kristmeier nodded slowly and put something special into his smile. 'You're onto those already are you? I thought that that might be what's rattled your cage. For as long as I knew them – ten years or more – the Doctor and his nephew have been going abroad, at their own expense, wherever they felt that the need was greatest – usually to a country struggling to recover from the aftermath of war. They never looked for any publicity and most people who heard about the trips were impressed by the deeds and by the modesty.'

'But you were not?' Honey suggested.

'No I was not.' Kristmeier's lip curled. 'I was always sure that there was something wrong. They were genuine medical trips and I made sure that any tax deduction claimed was valid and within the rules, and yet there were a dozen discordant elements. They were mostly tiny things and never anything one could take hold of except for my blind certainty that Dr McGordon was a trustworthy doctor but an untrustworthy man. Do you know what I mean?'

'Only too well. I've met a hundred of them. Who sent the pair of them out to wherever they went?' Honey asked. She glanced at Allan Dodson, who was glaring at the monitor screen. 'I mean, you can't just say to yourself, "I bet they could make use of my skills in Azerbaijan," and pack your bags and go and put up a brass plate or knock on the door of a clinic. There would have to be arrangements in advance or most of your time there would be wasted.'

Kristmeier smiled indulgently. 'Of course there would. They were sponsored by a surgical offshoot of *Médecin Sans Frontières*. Dr McGordon would do the diagnosis and medication while Mr Samson performed any surgery that was possible in the poor conditions. Sometime, if it wasn't possible on the spot, they'd bring the patient back with them.'

'I suppose,' Honey said, 'that they went very early in the year because colder weather would be less favourable to infections or to the insects that carry them.'

'Exactly. They not only paid for their own fares and accommodation but when they brought back a patient who needed treatment that they couldn't manage in the primitive conditions they paid for it themselves. I don't know what the treatment cost them – Dr McGordon was always careful to keep his dealings with the clinic to himself and out of my hands. That, if nothing else, seemed out of key because it was just the sort of thing that he should have expected me to deal with for him. What's more, I know that they never claimed tax relief on those patients' air fares. Yet neither of them ever seemed charitably inclined in any other way. I've even heard them exchanging *laithfu* jokes about poor patients.' The escape of the broad Scots word made Kristmeier hesitate.

When he resumed, his accent was more carefully neutral. 'Uncharitable, I mean. The kind of joke that would be denounced as politically incorrect.'

'The world might think their activities very commendable,' Honey said. Hope was being replaced by certainty and a beginning of triumph. Even the day outside the window was looking brighter. 'So might I have done. Except,' she said, 'that I had the radio on this morning and some member of the Godly was telling the old story about the elderly Spaniard who crossed into France every day by bicycle. The local customs officer was sure that he was smuggling something, but he searched him again and again and even took his bicycle to pieces and found nothing. So when the Spaniard was very old and on his deathbed the customs officer, who was now retired, went to see him and said, "You've nothing to lose now so please satisfy my curiosity. I know that you were smuggling and I can't think what. Please tell me." And the Spaniard smiled and said, "Bicycles." I forget what moral was drawn from the story. It's been ticking over in the back of my mind ever since and now I know why.'

The two men looked puzzled. 'And what moral do you draw from it?' Dodson asked.

'Were they smuggling people? Didn't the same person go back after the operation?'

'You're still not quite there. About the bringing back of patients for treatment in this country, what better way to smuggle body parts? I'd been thinking along the lines of refrigerated containers, but I'm sure that that wouldn't be practical and it would attract the attention of all the wrong officials.'

Harry Kristmeier snapped his fingers. 'That's the missing element,' he said. 'I should have thought of it.'

'I still don't understand,' Dodson said plaintively. 'Are body parts worth smuggling?'

Dodson was not usually so slow. Honey could see that half of his mind was wrestling with the problems posed by Mr Blackhouse's email. 'Look at it this way,' she said. 'There's a law in this country against buying or selling body parts. But imagine being a very rich person and you or somebody dear to you desperately needs a kidney to save his life. There's no relative suitable and willing to donate one and a long queue for donors. But just suppose that two doctors go to conduct clinics in the poorest country imaginable, somewhere where a war has just finished and people are starving. Those doctors keep a check on their patients, looking for somebody with a compatible kidney and in dire need of money to feed their family, pay the rent or buy a house or a bit of land. The doctors might even have taken a shopping list with them. How much do you suppose that rich person would be prepared to pay?'

Dodson had changed colour and his eyes were very wide. 'You mean that somebody might sell bits of himself? I don't believe it.'

'That's because you're young and innocent,' Honey said, 'and you've lived a comparatively prosperous life in the bosom of a protective family. When you watch the TV look hard at some of the news stories, at the aftermath of wars and earthquakes and famines, tsunamis and general damned incompetence and corruption. There are people out there who have literally nothing, who don't know where the next meal is coming from or how to provide for their children. Imagine yourself in that predicament and ask yourself whether you wouldn't give up a kidney, or anything else that you have two of, for enough to give you a fresh start, or even just to tide you over until things might, just might, change for the better.' She tried to keep her tone dispassionate but it was a subject that always touched her on the raw. What she never said aloud, even to Sandy, was that most of her allowance from Mr Potterton-Phipps went by direct debit to Oxfam.

'That was a kidney,' Kristmeier said. 'But eyes are even more difficult. They have to match for size and fit the socket. And preferably match for colour, although I suppose a coloured contact lens would do the trick. Think of a fabulously wealthy man who's losing his sight because of some congenital defect of the retina. What would he pay for a serviceable replacement?'

Honey was nodding. 'To a starving peasant, a sum that to us would seem comparatively trifling might be a lifeline to himself and his family. Compared to what a wealthy citizen in the West might pay, that would leave a very healthy mark-up for the two doctors to share between them. Totally illegal; and ethically, of course, making an enormous profit off a desperate man's body parts stinks to high Heaven. So,' Honey said, 'we have a possible scenario. But it's still no more than a theory, a possibility. No, let's call it a probability. To test it, we need to know the answers to three questions. One, what patients did the doctors bring back to this country? Two, did those visits coincide with transplant operations?

Three, were there payments into Dr McGordon's personal bank account later, at appropriate dates?'

Kristmeier gave an expressive shrug. 'Much though I'd love to uncover any shenanigans on Dr McGordon's part,' he said, 'I can't help you with the last one.'

Honey and Dodson exchanged glances. 'The bank accounts? You can leave that one to us,' Honey said. 'Can you help with the first two?'

'I think so. I'm told that the computer system that I set up is still up and running, so they haven't brought in a new manager, just a senior receptionist and bookkeeper. There's a link between the computer at Dr McGordon's surgery and the one at the Gilberton Clinic, so that he can read his case-notes wherever he is at the time. If – and I don't think that it's too big an if,' Kristmeier said thoughtfully, '– if they haven't rewritten the computer codes, I can get details of the operations. I'm not sure whether the donors brought into the country masquerading as patients would be listed.'

'They might very well not be travelling under their own names and passports,' Honey said.

'True. But I think that I could persuade

Donna Michelet to help me out. She's the executive at the agency that arranged the foreign trips.'

'You know her well?'

'I think you could say that,' Kristmeier said. There was a touch of complacency in his manner that made Honey want to slap him, an absolute confidence that this woman or any other would still be so enamoured of him that she would do his bidding. 'She comes over to interview surgeons and doctors about twice a year. We used to meet.' The feminist streak in Honey was deeply buried but he was jerking it to the surface. He still exuded sexual magnetism but she found his self-satisfaction a total turn-off. She was careful not to show any signs of disenchantment. She needed him. She didn't have to like him as well.

Honey was sure that there was one more avenue to explore. It had entered her mind while they spoke but after a long period of near stagnation events were now moving so quickly that she had to pause and struggle to recall what it might be. It came to her at last. 'You know Ms Michelet well enough to get details of the donors' progress after their return to their own countries? I'm going to need it tomorrow.'

'This is where we come to the bigger ifs,' Kristmeier said. 'If she's in her office and not travelling tomorrow and if they retain that sort of information and if she hasn't forgotten dear old Harry Kristmeier, then there's a chance. The time difference could help. You'll pay for a call to France? Is it important? It could be a long call, to Paris.'

'I don't think she'll have forgotten you,' Honey said before she could stop herself. She went on in a hurry. 'Yes, it could be very important and I'll see that you get reimbursed for the call, however long it takes. I suggest that you two work in liaison and try to find the answers to those questions. Meanwhile, I'll prepare a report on what progress we've been able to make so far and I'll trawl through all that's gone before in the hope of spotting whatever we've missed.'

'You think we've missed something?' Dodson asked.

'I'm damn sure we've missed something,' said Honey. 'In hindsight, you always find that you've missed something.'

She let Dodson see Kristmeier out. When the PC returned he said, 'We're meeting later today, when we've gathered up what we need. You're going to have an exciting morning on Tuesday.'

241

'So are you,' Honey said. 'I'll want you standing by. You're the only witness who can say that Mr Blackhouse ever told me to investigate Dr McGordon.'

## Chapter Seventeen

Honey spent a largely restless night, fruitlessly reviewing possible scenarios for the coming day's activity and Tuesday's meeting. She could see disastrous possibilities ahead. Quite apart from the termination of her career, she might even be vulnerable in criminal law for participating in breaches of the Data Protection Act. The only conclusion that she arrived at was that if Detective Superintendent Blackhouse did indeed try to climb out of the mess by way of her shoulders she would spare no effort to climb out via his. In the small hours she fell suddenly asleep, waking after her usual time, thick headed and alone. She rose too quickly, sat with her head tilted back until it cleared and then dragged on a dressing gown.

She found Sandy already dressed as if for golf and lingering with the morning paper over the remains of a hearty breakfast. 'I let you sleep,' he said. 'You've plenty of time to prepare for your meeting tomorrow.'

Honey found herself pulled in different directions. She was touched by his consideration and annoyed that valuable time had been wasted. She managed what she hoped was an affectionate grunt. 'You may as well go and play golf,' she said.

'Have you looked outside?'

Honey looked out of the window for the first time. Fog had closed in. 'Not nice,' she said.

'Very much not nice. Can I help at all?'

'Probably not, but if you're going to be at home I shan't hesitate to call on you. How's that?'

'That's acceptable. Just don't overdo it. And don't worry.'

That, Honey decided, was all very well. There was a very vague line between profitless worrying and profitable thought; and it could be impossible to tell them apart until after the event. Her sleepless worrying during the small hours had probably been of the unprofitable variety and yet there was an idea trying to form in the back of her mind. Something she herself had said almost casually...

She carried a cup of tea and a bowl of cereal through to the study and looked for emails. Among the junk mail was a message from Allan Dodson.

*The unexplained payments correspond approximately with the dates of returns from abroad plus a month or two. I have a list of possible recipients and another of donors; I think they match up. Kristmeier has been in touch with his contact who confirms the identities of patients brought back to this country. She will try to trace their subsequent histories and call him back. He has to go to work today and he can't take phone calls there so he gave her your phone number. I am looking for payments that may coincide.*

Honey was perturbed to see such damning material committed to a medium that would be all too permanent and accessible to hostile superiors. On the other hand, it seemed that things were beginning to move. Perhaps they were already past the point at which caution was useful. Should she try to profit from vague and unsubstantiated allegations? Perhaps it would it be safer to say, 'Yes, Sir, Mr Blackhouse did suggest that I investigate the Doctor but I had my doubts as to whether that constituted a valid order and in view of my delicate condition I did nothing about it.' As a defence it would be of doubtful value, might be easily disproved and would be disloyal in the extreme. Perhaps Sandy's suggestion was the best, that she skip the meeting altogether and see what came out of it. And yet, at some time in every quandary came the moment of no return, the time when the odds favoured continued attack rather than defence. A constable had once, in her hearing, used the expression *Shit or bust!* She had given him a good tongue-lashing but even at the time she had known that it was more for carelessness in failing to notice the presence of a superior officer rather than for the words themselves. She now thought that she understood the meaning.

Before returning upstairs to prepare herself for the day, she visited the kitchen and found June performing her endless cleaning and tidying. 'This is urgent,' Honey told her. 'I want to know what the Doctor's mood is. Can you get hold of your pal next door?'

'I think so,' June said. 'She said that we must get together again. I'll phone her.'

'Do that. I want to know if the Doctor's still happy and confident. Does he show signs of worry? This could help you towards your holiday.'

Honey retired upstairs to wash, dress and make up for the day. When she came down again she could hear June's voice. From the short sentences and silences she knew that June was on the phone. When the sounds of the phone call ended, June appeared in the study doorway.

'She's coming round for a cup of tea this afternoon,' she said.

'Not until then?'

June shrugged. 'Best I could do. I suggested that I was having a quiet day and she'd be welcome to have coffee here or I could come round to her. She didn't seem to want me to go round there but said that she could join me here.'

'You got the impression that something was happening?'

'I think so.'

With that, Honey had to be content for the moment. She settled on the couch and told herself that every great leader had had to learn how to relax and let others do their delegated tasks. She had just decided that such detachment was not possible for one of her disposition and that, but for her pregnancy, she would have been out there, rushing around and getting in the way, when to her later surprise she fell asleep. Her restless night was overtaking her.

She was woken by the sound of the telephone. June would usually insist on answering it and informing Honey who was on the line; but June had quite enough to do and she could see reasons for keeping her telephone traffic as confidential as possible. She fumbled muzzily on the occasional table beside her and lifted the phone before June could dash to the instrument in the hall.

The voice that greeted her had a French accent so strong that it almost belonged on the stage, though it was soon evident that the speaker's English was rather better than Honey's French, so English was the preferred language.

''Allo. Is that Madame Laird who speaks?'

'It is,' Honey said.

'And you are an officer of the police, yes?'

'That's so,' said Honey. 'I am taking calls at home because I am pregnant – *enceinte,* is that right? – and my baby is due. If you are in any doubt you can check my identity by–'

Even the laugh at the other end had a distinctly French accent. 'That will not be necessary. My good friend Harry Kristmeier spoke for you. I am Donna Michelet. My friend Harry gave me your number to call.' At every mention of Kristmeier her voice softened. 'This is important?' she asked.

'Very important,' said Honey.

'Harry says that you wish to know of the progress of the patients who the good Doctor McGordon treated in Scotland. It will take some time because they have returned to their own countries, different countries you understand, and sometimes the time difference will make delay. The matter is urgent?'

'Very.'

'It is difficult to understand what business this is of the police.' *Shit or bust,* Honey told herself. Even so, she chose her words with care. 'It is a question concerning the honesty and integrity of certain medical staff. I beg you to accept that it is so.'

There was a pause at the other end of the line. Honey thought that she might be coming up against the Anglophobia and obstruction for which the French are famous. But apparently she was wronging Madame – or Mademoiselle – Michelet. 'I will do what I can. You will be at that telephone all day?'

'I'll give you my mobile number.' Honey quoted it. 'You can reach me on that at any time. Please give me yours... And a thousand thanks.'

One anxious hour later the phone rang again. Honey snatched it up. Dodson was on the line. 'Inspector, we have a good correlation between patients being brought back to Britain, operations in the Gilberton Clinic, patients returning to their home countries and money reaching the Doctor's bank account. There will have been some imaginative recording of medical details because the nature of the operation doesn't always correspond exactly with the condition recorded for the patient. One woman, for instance, was brought from Afghanistan for surgical removal of infected ovaries. A few days later a patient of Dr McGordon's received a kidney transplant. There's no word of a donor, dead or alive.'

'That's good enough,' Honey said. 'Or at least it's the best that we've any right to expect. Tabulate what we've got and let me have it.'

The day dragged onward. Honey ate a light lunch. Then, while June entertained Mrs Deakin, she and Sandy took Pippa for a gentle walk, remembering to carry her mobile phone both charged and switched on. Leaning on her husband's arm and encouraged by a sudden improvement in the weather, she managed a longer walk than she was accustomed to. They were near the top of the hill and admiring the view across the Forth to Fife when her mobile suddenly played its little tune, the clog dance from *La fille mal gardee*.

Donna Michelet was on the line. 'I have much of what you want,' she said. 'Of the Doctor's patients one has died, but he had a heart disease and was not expected to live. The Doctor's efforts must have been of desperation. The others progress well but with one exception. There was a man from Bosnia. I am told that he lives still but I have difficulty hearing any more. There is secrecy about his progress.'

Honey and her husband exchanged a look. 'Could you make a guess,' Honey asked, 'as to why they are being so secretive?'

During the momentary silence Honey could envisage a Gallic shrug. 'It is something legal, that is all I know. I have tried all I can but there is a barrier.'

'Thank you,' Honey said. 'Thank you very much.'

'We'd better go back to the house,' Sandy said. 'I may be able to find out something over the police network but I need a proper phone and my book of numbers.'

Sandy left his wife to make her own way from the corner of the Doctor's garden while he hurried ahead to use the phone.

Honey arrived home, relieved to have managed to walk without allowing Pippa to roll in anything worse than straw. Sandy's voice could be heard from the study but there were no voices to be heard from the kitchen. Honey looked in. June was putting away the teacups but she poured a fresh cup of tea for her mistress. Mrs Deakin, she said, had hurried back next door.

Honey draped her coat over a chair and sat down. 'What did you get?' she asked.

'I'm no' sure,' June said. 'Mrs Deakin didn't seem too sure herself. She hadn't felt that she could stay out too long because the Doctor had been like a cat on hot bricks. She thought that some packing might be in train because every now and again he would call on Mrs Deakin to produce some half forgotten item, but he never let her see what he was packing. And no, he hadn't said anything about going away, but the dogs behaved as if they knew that he was going, and then he went off in the car with the two dogs and came back without them, just as he did when he went off on his foreign trips.'

'Thank you,' Honey said slowly. 'That's very interesting.'

'Do I get my holiday?'

'It seems very likely.'

Honey had to wait some time before Sandy came off the phone. He joined her in the sitting room. 'I couldn't go through anybody local,' he said, 'but I have a pal in Strathclyde who owes me a favour and he has a pal in Bosnia who's going to find out about it and call me.'

Honey greeted the news with a kiss to Sandy's left ear. 'Now that that's as settled as it can be for the moment,' Honey said, 'here's another news item. The Doctor's housekeeper thinks he may be planning another sudden trip abroad although he hasn't said anything to her. Would it be in my best interests to let him do a runner? Or should we prepare to pull him in?'

'I'm going to have a dram while I think about it. Too bad about you.' Sandy poured himself a generous ration of very good malt. Clearly he had thought to some purpose. He rejoined his wife on the settee and pulled her back against him. 'It's a temptation. We could put a car outside his house and another at his nephew's, to pull them in if they head for an airport. But that would put you immediately in the wrong. And just suppose that it turned out that their medical trip for this year had been brought forward and he hadn't got round to telling Mrs Deakin yet. No, I think we have to let him go and then put the blame squarely where it belongs.'

## Chapter Eighteen

Honey might have spent another restless night but Sandy, recognising the symptoms, had slipped half a sleeping tablet into her milky drink. Any problem is far greater to the person likely to be affected but Honey left it all behind and slept deeply and dreamlessly. She woke slightly fuddled but her head soon cleared and she congratulated herself on having risen above her anxieties.

She found Sandy already dressed for the office 'I let you sleep,' he said. 'You've plenty of time before your meeting.'

'I think I'll need all of it.' She helped herself to a mug of tea.

'You'd better have something solid and some sugar.'

Honey did not feel in the least like anything solid. She rather thought that her worries were giving her an ulcer. However, she might well need sustenance before her ordeal was over, one way or the other, and something milky might be good for an ulcer. She took a bowl of cereal and carried it through to the study. There was an email from Dodson.

*Kristmeier's contact has been in touch with him. Some rumblings at the Kosovo end have got back to her and she wants to know what's going on. He says she can wait a day or two. I have the tabulation you wanted. I will meet you near the ACC's office.*

Her mind was not yet in fully active mode but experience told her that it would wake up at the same pace as the rest of her. Anything that she did or thought now would only find an uncertain resting-place in her memory. She decided to get ready for the day before gearing up for thinking.

She climbed the stairs, took a shower and began to think about clothes. The men would probably be in dark suits. The leading designers were now turning their attention to maternity wear so that her own range of choice was only slightly circumscribed by her pregnancy and was much wider than a man's but would also be more revealing. She wanted to look good but at the same time to appear strong and not a supplicant, certainly not like somebody who would accept being pushed around. Too much dark formality might look funereal, as if she were already condemned. But too much colour would look frivolous. A suit would have been best, but she could no longer get into any of her suit skirts. From among her purchases of maternity wear by top designers and those passed on by her sisters-in-law, she chose one of navy blue with a pale pattern and a deep neck, and she allied it to a pale pink blouse. Some jewellery, but very little. She brushed out her hair and gave thanks that she had visited the hairdresser just before Mr Blackhouse's visit. Her natural waves would do the rest of the job for her. She made up with care, making allowance for the fluorescent lights that were common through the offices.

She had time for a phone call. Her intention was to contact Allan Dodson for more details than were revealed in his email. To retain a record, she attached her tape recorder to the phone. At that moment the phone rang, making her jump. She picked up the receiver.

'Mrs Laird? Or should I say Detective Inspector Laird?'

If the accent had been any one of the many local accents to be found in Scotland she might have had difficulty in picking out individual tones, but within the combination of a raised voice with the neutral accent of the educated Scot she could hear echoes of the Doctor's authoritative voice. A guess at the identity would do no harm if wrong. She kept control of her own voice. 'Either will do, Mr Samson?'

There was a momentary silence that she thought denoted shock. This in turn suggested that he had not intended to reveal his identity. The person intending an anonymous phone call must, she thought, feel very naked when addressed by name. He made a quick recovery. 'So you know my voice. Have you been tapping my phone?'

Honey felt a momentary dizziness and a fresh twinge somewhere below her midriff. She concentrated on keeping her voice calm and steady. 'Certainly not. That would be most improper. Was that what you wanted to ask me? The answer is no. What else can I do for you, Mr Samson?'

'You can stop looking into my affairs and those of my uncle. You've been poking your pretty little nose in where it isn't wanted. And against very definite orders to the contrary.'

Any idea of being conciliatory went straight out of the window. Honey felt her hackles rise. Her breath quickened but her

256

voice remained calm. 'And how do you come to know anything about orders given to the police, Mr Samson?' she asked.

'Never you mind how I know. I do know. And I know a lot more. I know that you're going to be told very firmly from on high to lay off. And I know that if you disobey that order again you'll be a very sorry girl. I'm warning you, leave me alone. If you poke that pretty nose in any more you could lose it. And how would you look to your baby after that?'

'You seem to be suggesting a surgical operation,' Honey said as calmly as she could manage. 'How do you think the Ethical Committee will look on it?'

'I ... I'm not suggesting anything of the sort. This isn't a consultation. I'm just warning you.' The connection was suddenly broken.

Honey hung up and sat breathing deeply for some seconds. She told herself that nothing had changed. On the whole, she thought that she had had the better of the exchange. Then it came to her that something very definitely had changed. She had no recollection of starting the tape recorder but she saw that the reels were turning. When she wound it back, she found that she had a recording of the Doctor's threats. She found herself grinning. That, surely, should help to convince the ACC (Crime) that something was far wrong. She put the cassette carefully into an envelope.

The day outside had turned into one of those perfect winter's days of sunshine and blue sky that promise, usually without any semblance to the truth, that springtime will soon come around. But it also looked very cold. She was choosing a wraparound tweed coat when Sandy appeared beside her. 'You still have time in hand,' he said.

'I'm meeting Dodson to find out what he and Kristmeier have got.'

'All right. I'll drive you.'

'June could do that.'

He smiled. 'June will be busy.'

'Sandy,' she said, 'you have things to do and you can't spare time to nursemaid me when I've let Mr Blackhouse persuade me to put my head beside his on the block. Now I have to stand or fall by my own wits. I don't want to take you away from your own things–'

He put an arm around her shoulders and gave her a quick hug. 'Can't you see that I want to drive you? I waited for you. I want you to see that you have my support all the way. Also I haven't heard back about the patient in Kosovo yet. I'll call you on your mobile or get a note taken in to you if anything helpful turns up.'

She was touched. She returned his hug. 'Thank you, darling. I do appreciate it and I accept your kind offer of support in the spirit in which I hope it's meant. Shall we go?'

'Don't you want any papers with you?'

'I've been over them so often that I know them by heart.' And if she carried papers into the meeting she could no longer pretend that she had taken no action.

Sandy took the Range Rover because Honey found it more comfortable than his Vectra. They drove in silence through streets that looked grey in spite of the sunshine. He parked near the main entrance. 'Would you like me to come in with you? You'd be quite entitled to have a more senior officer to advise you or to speak up for you.'

She kissed his cheek. He was perfectly shaved. 'Bless you, but no. That would make me look guilty before I began.'

'All right.' He dabbed at his cheek to make sure that she had not left a lipstick mark. 'Mind that you don't get stressed – it would be bad tactics and it wouldn't do you or the baby much good. I'll be in the office preparing a brief for counsel for most of the day, but my mobile will be switched on. Phone me as soon as you're ready or if you need me and I'll come for you.'

As she walked to the door, she felt choked with emotion. She seemed to be developing a nervous stomach. She told herself not to be ridiculous. She was not going to the guillotine. The worst that could happen would be dismissal; more likely would be a reprimand and some loss of seniority. Even that was improbable, if it was accepted that she had been instructed by her superior officer. It was even possible that Mr Blackhouse would suffer a forced retirement and his post be offered to Sandy. She toyed with the dream during the ride in the lift but she knew that a husband and wife working in such close harness would not be acceptable. And how far if at all, she wondered again, would Mr Blackhouse go to exonerate her? He had taken one of his inexplicable likings to her but he was not noted for loyalty and consideration towards his juniors.

The lift discharged her at an unfamiliar floor, distinguished by a decor which, though not more expensive than elsewhere in the building, was more carefully chosen. The corridor was empty. She was about to start reading the names on the doors when her attention was attracted by a low hiss. A small recess opposite the lifts held four chairs and Allan Dodson was trying to attract her attention. He was seated, with a disintegrating batch of papers on one knee while he tried to write on the other. She sat beside him. A seated position seemed to have become more comfortable than standing.

'Progress, Inspector,' he said softly. 'Quite a lot of it.' He produced a double sheet of typing paper almost covered with small blocks of his neat writing. He was smiling. Honey looked closely at him to judge whether the smile was forced. 'Some of this is guesswork but the dates seem to fit. I thought it safer not to put headings to the columns, so you'll have to remember them. The first column gives the dates of the two doctors' foreign trips. The next shows the name of anyone they brought back with them. Two of the spaces in that column are blank, so they didn't find any matching kidneys or other bits or pieces in those years. On the other hand, three times they came back accompanied by more than one person. Once, one of those was the recipient, an Arab prince receiving a testicle from one of his staff.' Allan paused and she perceived a half concealed look of pain on his face. 'A reluctant volunteer, I suspect. That time, Dr McGordon made the reservations but the prince paid the fares.

'The third column gives the date and nature of an operation following immediately after their return. In the fourth column, I've listed the dates and amounts of large, unexplained credits to the Doctor's bank account. Those facts in the fourth column are in pencil. That's so that you can rub out that particular information if necessary or if it turns out to be irrelevant. The information was not obtained in a manner that I would want to speak about in court. You have an eraser?' he asked anxiously.

'I do understand,' she said. She accepted an India rubber from him and stowed it in the pocket of her maternity dress. 'You seem to be thinking on your feet,' she added.

'Thank you. I'm learning from you. The last column is blank. It was intended to hold the later history of the donors. Kristmeier is still hoping to hear back from his contact. If he calls me, I'll get a note to you somehow.'

'He phoned me,' Honey said. 'I have all the information, or as much as he would give me. There's one offbeat one that nobody wants to talk about and I'm hoping that there's a reason for it. Word should reach me during the meeting.'

'Then I think that's as far as we can go.'

'You've done very well,' Honey said. 'You're wasted in Traffic. Thank you. Whatever happens, I won't drop you or your friend in it.' She touched the back of his hand. She was aware of another mild stomach-ache. Surely she couldn't really be developing an ulcer? Perhaps a touch of indigestion. The moment passed.

'It's me that owes you thanks.' Dodson's usually reliable grammar was slipping under pressure of emotion. 'I'll tell you something, Inspector, about yesterday. I owe you. I can go back to clay pigeons now, knowing that it isn't an end in itself but it's practice for something real.' He sighed. 'I can't explain the attraction. It's not the thrill of killing something. I've shot rats in a barn before now and it didn't mean a thing. A big game-bird coming fast, that's something else. You look at it and you know that it's good meat. So you say to it, "I want you". And you swing through quickly and pull the trigger and if you've got it right it turns over in the air and comes down with a meaty thump. And then ... then I watched your dog pick it up and come back looking so proud and happy that... I don't have the words for it.'

'You're not doing badly,' Honey said, smiling. 'If you're really keen, I could maybe fix you up with a keeper, helping him out and acting as a beater. That usually gets you a day or two at the pheasants at the end of the season–'

She was interrupted by the appearance of Mrs Marrack, the retired former woman sergeant who acted as secretary and receptionist for the ACC (Crime). She had a bulldog face and a reputation for ferocity. It was said that when she first arrived in the ranks of the uniformed branch there had soon been a measurable drop in the Edinburgh crime figures, largely because many of the criminals had moved back to Glasgow. It was further said that police attack dogs cowered away from her and that, when the day of her retirement arrived, she had obtained her present post simply because nobody had dared to turn her down.

'You're here, Inspector Laird?' she snapped. 'They're waiting for you.'

Honey looked at her watch. 'It isn't eleven yet. I'm not late.'

'That doesn't prevent them waiting for you. Come.'

Honey grabbed the pages that Dodson

pushed towards her and followed at heel. Mrs Marrack walked like a marching guardsman. Her grooming was so rigidly disciplined that she made Honey feel that her own careful toilet was slovenly. Honey expected her ulcer to flare again but it remained dormant. Her mind was too busy turning over the available facts to take in her surroundings, but eventually a door was opened, Mrs Marrack announced her name and she found herself in an austere room, but she was aware of walking onto a softer carpet. Mrs Marrack took her coat from her and hung it up with a consideration that had become almost motherly. Honey left Dodson's paper in the pocket.

'May I leave my mobile phone with you?' she asked. 'There may be a message for me.'

Mrs Marrack nodded and left the room, carrying Honey's mobile with care.

There were three men in the room. The two men on the far side of the big desk remained seated but Mr Blackhouse, whose back had been towards her and who would usually be the last person to think of offering courtesy to a subordinate, stood and, at a nod from across the desk, even held her chair for her.

Honey's encounters with Mr Holland, the

ACC(Crime), had been limited to his presence during a promotion interview and later a duty dance following a staff dinner. His was not, at first glance, a threatening figure. He was rather small for a profession that still tends to favour the burly and he had a face that in repose was almost kindly. It was looking serious now, but he had the reputation of being fair and working by the book.

He introduced his depute, who Honey had not previously met. Mr Vosp was still in his thirties, substantially younger than his chief, lean and hawk-faced with a head of thin, prematurely greying hair. His eyes were hooded and his face seemed to be set in an almost permanent sneer. He was looking at her in a way that she found hard to interpret but she could be sure that it was not friendly. Honey knew immediately that if there were to be trouble he would be the source of it.

Mr Holland spoke first. 'This is not a formal disciplinary hearing but a preliminary, fact-gathering meeting. Disciplinary hearings may follow. You understand?'

'I understand,' Honey said.

'The discussion is being recorded and a copy of the tape will be available to you. I should tell you first that Mr Blackhouse has already been interviewed. He accepts that he instructed you to investigate your neighbour, Dr McGordon, despite receiving orders to the contrary.' Mr Holland paused before resuming. 'Did you in fact proceed with the investigation.'

Honey had made her mind up. 'Yes,' she said.

'Knowing that your instructions had been given against orders?'

Honey looked at Mr Blackhouse. He was not looking in her direction but she knew that she was visible in the corner of his eye. She could still cover herself at his expense. But his attitude, often that of a bully, was now, whether he knew it or not, one of pathos. She did not have to like him to have sympathy for him. 'Yes,' she said.

The two senior men exchanged a glance. 'I think that that's all that we need to know,' Mr Vosp said briskly.

'May I ask a question?' Honey enquired gently.

The two men looked surprised but Mr Holland said, 'Go ahead.'

'Would it make any difference to the outcome if I were to tell you that I did arrive at a conclusion.'

'In my opinion, no,' Mr Vosp said. 'This

meeting was called in order to decide whether orders had been disobeyed. We now know the answer.'

Mr Blackhouse sat up straight. Honey's support seemed to have stiffened his backbone. 'You are implying that there is never any excuse for acting against orders. But, with all respect, that is the kind of argument that has been put up by every minor war criminal since the Nuremberg Trials. It has become clear that orders are no excuse for wrong behaviour. If the order was wrong and should never have been given, then there was justification for ignoring it.'

Mr Vosp drew himself up. 'In this instance, the orders were clear and legitimate. I resent any suggestion that they were in any way improper.'

'Superintendent Blackhouse has a point,' Mr Holland said. 'It's certainly an argument that would better be considered at this early stage. Let the inspector tell us what she uncovered.'

'Off the record,' Mr Vosp suggested.

'I would object to that,' Honey said.

Blackhouse grunted agreement. 'So would I.'

'Let's have a complete record,' said Mr Holland. 'We don't want any suggestion of a cover-up. Carry on, Inspector.'

'Thank you. You'll appreciate,' Honey said, 'that working from home with no backup, no facilities and no access to official records I could not possibly arrive at a case that would stand up in court. But I am absolutely confident that continued investigation along the same lines will produce a proven case.

'Dr McGordon and his nephew, Mr Samson, who is a surgeon, have been in the habit of going abroad to give free medical aid in impoverished countries.'

'Nothing wrong with that,' Vosp snapped. 'That fact is well known.'

'Of course,' Honey said. 'But on most such trips they brought back a patient with them who subsequently underwent surgery in the Gilberton Clinic.' Honey was only too well aware that she would soon run out of evidence that she could produce. The Doctor's bank statements, for instance, had been obtained by means that would be far outside the law. The records from Dr McGordon's medical office were similarly taboo, but more or less so? Her stomach-ache had returned, more insistent. She was tempted to ask whether any of the men had a Rennie. 'May I play you a piece of tape?' she enquired.

'I see no reason why not,' said the ACC. He produced a cassette recorder from a bottom drawer of the desk. Honey played the recording of the telephone call. As she pressed the key she became aware that her hand was shaking. The three men listened to the voices in silence except for an occasional small sound of surprise or – dared she hope? – disapproval.

'That doesn't mean a thing,' Vosp said. 'What Mr Samson told you on the phone is much what you'd been told through Mr Blackhouse.'

'Except,' said Mr Holland, 'that Mr Samson was not authorised to make any such threatening remarks and he does seem to have been in possession of information that should never have left this building. We will have to consider both aspects with care but together they come very close to an attempt to pervert the course of justice, wouldn't you say?'

'No, I would not,' Mr Vosp snapped. With respect, Mr Holland, there is not a single threat on that tape; only warnings of consequences that Inspector Laird over-reacted to and seemed and still seems to be bringing on herself. The reference to losing her nose was merely the kind of colloquialism that gets

270

resorted to when discussions get heated.'

The ACC(Crime) looked at his depute for a few seconds before continuing. 'Except that he went on to refer to the effect that that – um – amputation would have on her baby. That suggests that the threat was literal rather than figurative. But we'll consider the implications later. Go ahead, Inspector.'

Honey ignored another grumble from her midriff. 'May I have my cassette back, please? You do have a copy of it in the record now.'

Vosp flared up again. 'Are you daring to imply that the tape might be tampered with?'

'The tape is Inspector Laird's property,' said Mr Holland tiredly. 'As she says, we now have a copy.' He ejected the cassette and handed it across the desk. 'Now, Inspector.'

'I have good reason to believe–' Honey resumed.

There came a peremptory rap at the door and Mrs Marrack entered. 'There is a phone call for Inspector Laird from one of the chief inspectors,' she said. 'He insisted that it was urgent.'

'It could have waited until after the meeting,' said Vosp.

Mrs Marrack pierced him with a quelling eye. 'He said not,' she retorted. Turning away, she exchanged glances with Honey and – miracle of miracles! – there was the suggestion of a wink.

There would be time later to wonder whether Mrs Marrack was expressing sympathy out of dislike for Mr Vosp or because of a closing of feminist ranks. Honey listened to Sandy's voice on the phone and relief swelled alongside the baby inside her. It was followed by a nervous spasm. Good news for herself and Mr Blackhouse would be disaster for others. Her stomach was cramping but she gritted her teeth. 'This is what I was waiting for,' she said. 'This is convincing.'

All three men were throwing questions at her but she stuck to her own agenda. She spoke quickly, ignoring the cramps in her stomach. 'I now have reason to believe that the so-called patients who came to Britain with the two doctors were in fact donors who had come to sell their own organs for transplant.' She paused and gritted her teeth against a passing spasm. 'That, of course, is illegal. But it becomes much more serious. I now have information about the last such person–'

She broke off. She had another and overriding concern. They were staring at her but that hardly mattered. She realised that she was sitting in a puddle. She opened her mobile phone again and keyed in the short code for Sandy's number.

'I'm sorry about your chair,' she told the ACC(Crime). Sandy answered his mobile. 'Come and get me,' she said. 'Hurry, hurry, hurry. My water's broken.'

## Chapter Nineteen

That same afternoon Sandy sat at his wife's bedside, holding her hand while snatching occasional glances into the cot at the foot of the bed where his brand new daughter was sleeping. The midwives agreed that it had been one of the quickest and easiest births in memory. This, they had also agreed, had been because the main participant had seemed to be thinking about something else. The maternity home had been only a five-minute journey by ambulance so that labour, which had already started when the ambulance set out, was still incomplete on arrival. It had lasted for all of a further twenty minutes. Honey recalled the experience as having been painful but not agonising; indeed, the memory of the pain was fading already. She was not even particularly tired but she was relieved to be rid of the extra weight and to be assured that she was nursing a real baby and not an incipient ulcer.

A nurse came round the door. Despite the flattering uniform she was unprepossessing, having buck teeth and spots. 'There are three men asking to see you,' she said. 'They said they're policemen,' she added doubtfully.

'Then it's probably true,' Honey said. She was revelling in the fulfilment of motherhood and delighted that both the discomfort of labour and her responsibility in the matter of Dr McGordon were coming to an end. She could feel the beginning of a return of the flippancy that she had thought was gone forever.

Sandy gave the nurse a reproving headshake. 'You may care to know,' he said, 'that my wife is a detective inspector, I'm a chief inspector and the three visitors are almost certainly the Assistant Chief Constable (Crime), his deputy and a detective superintendent. You have under your roof the cream of criminal investigation for Edinburgh and the whole of Lothian and Borders.'

'You, my boy, are getting above yourself,' Honey said. 'All the same, it's true. And this would not be a good time to tell them to go and bowl their hoops. You may as well let them in.' She crossed her bed-jacket carefully. Now that the bump was reduced almost to disappearing, her bosom seemed to have become disproportionately pro- nounced. She glanced at the side table where her tape recorder was waiting.

The three men came in and arranged themselves around the foot of the bed and therefore round the cot. The room, tricked out in tasteful colours and as much soft fabric as was compatible with hygiene, made every effort to seem unlike a hospital room. The visitors were noticeably un- comfortable; as well they might, Honey thought, in what was essentially matriarchal territory after all the fuss and accusations. Mr Blackhouse felt obliged to make the customary cooing noises over the infant; the ACC(Crime) contented himself with a clucking sound and his depute tried to look as though the whole business of procreation was far beneath his notice.

'So this is my goddaughter!' Mr Black- house announced, thus making a grab for moral ascendancy over the others. 'What is her name to be?'

'We haven't decided yet,' Sandy said. 'Suggestions would be welcomed.'

'We have business to conclude first,' Mr Holland said. 'Detective Inspector Laird was about to tell us her conclusions.'

'We really should not be troubling Mrs Laird at such a time,' his depute said anxiously.

'That's very considerate but you've already troubled me by throwing accusations around,' Honey pointed out. 'I'm just trying, if I can put it that way, to untrouble myself. You accused me of disobeying orders. But Mr Blackhouse and I found the Constable's story convincing. We decided to test it. There could be no reason not to do so except for somebody's desire to protect a friend or relative. Which was the more wicked – disobeying that order or trying to protect a friend from the consequences of a possible crime?'

The air in the room seemed to be filled with tension. Even the baby felt it. She awoke and made small sounds signifying interest.

'Surely,' Sandy said, 'this could have waited at least until my ... until Inspector Laird gets home.'

'That was my fault,' Mr Blackhouse said.

'I insisted. I didn't feel that either of us should be kept in suspense any longer.'

That note of apology was so unusual in the Detective Superintendent that Honey, overcome suddenly by maternal feelings towards the whole world, felt an urge to protect him. 'It couldn't have waited,' she said. 'I'm given to understand that Dr McGordon and his nephew are booked to go on another surgical safari very shortly. Let us by all means clear it up. When we do, I think you'll see why we shouldn't waste time, because what has happened before might well happen again. And, by the way, I do feel that this should still go on the record so I asked my husband to hurry home and fetch my cassette recorder. I'm sure that you have no objection.'

'We have every objection,' said Mr Vosp. 'This is all very irregular.'

The ACC (Crime) looked sharply at his depute. 'No, it isn't,' he said. Mr Vosp looked thunderous but remained silent.

Honey nodded to Sandy, who started the tape. 'I was telling you,' she said, 'that Dr McGordon and his nephew brought back patients when returning from most of their trips abroad. That much is public knowledge and has gained them considerable respect. Only it now seems that these were not patients but donors. You'll be aware that to buy body parts is illegal in this country. Smuggling body parts, or even importing them at all, is fraught with difficulties. The length of time that they are out of a donor's living body reduces proportionately the chance of a successful implant; and during that time they have to be kept cold, which would add enormously to the difficulty of smuggling. But a very wealthy man in need of an eye or a kidney, or in one instance a testicle –, (all three men flinched) '– will pay very handsomely for such a part, while a peasant with a starving family may sell one of a pair of components for a sum that may seem trifling to us but lifesaving to him.

'Dr McGordon has also gained credit in the eyes of the public by giving his services free to a clinic in the poorest part of Edinburgh. No doubt organs were also solicited through that source, but nobody is allowed to starve in Britain. In parts of Africa, the Middle East and the Americas, starving may at times be almost mandatory. And what better way to smuggle the part than in the living body of the donor?

'As I've already said, I don't have a case that would stand up in court. How could I possibly, without support or access to records and without court orders to open bank accounts? But I was fortunate in making contact, indirectly, with an official of the charitable body that organises surgery by visiting doctors and surgeons in impoverished countries. And by happy chance the Constable who was my sole help has a certain knack with young ladies. This he used to good effect in the Doctor's preferred travel agency, so that we have a list of places and dates of travel.'

Mr Holland seemed amused. 'Perhaps we should be schooling our younger and more attractive PCs in the art of gentle persuasion,' he said.

Sandy chuckled. 'I'm sure that my wife is more than competent to organise such a course,' he said.

'I'm sorry to spoil the party,' Honey said stiffly, 'but this really isn't funny. I would have been ready to laugh with you but for one factor. Let me explain. The official who organised the trips insists that, so far as she was aware, with only two exceptions the persons accompanying the two medical men back to Scotland were patients. The only exceptions were the very wealthy sheikh and the donor of the testicle.' Seeing all three men flinch, Honey could not resist disturbing their peace of mind a little further. 'The donor was said to be a willing volunteer but one has one's doubts. He may have given offence in some way and have been purging his contempt.'

She glanced around their faces. There could be no doubt that the idea of being conscripted to offer a testicle to an overlord struck at the heart of some deep, male instinct.

She resumed. 'The organisation, however, does keep in touch with patients whenever possible. In the most recent instance, almost a year ago, the patient, a Mr Yussuf Osman, was ostensibly brought to Britain for a kidney operation. In a sense that was true. He did indeed have a diseased kidney, which should have been removed. It has since emerged that his good kidney was the one that was removed, leaving Mr Osman's health seriously compromised. His home and the family farm are more than a hundred miles over mountainous roads from the nearest place where he could obtain dialysis, so you will see that his prospects are not good. It is now emerging that he was told nothing of the state of his kidney. Lawyers engaged on his behalf by his government have been in touch with the organisation, which has in turn contacted the Doctor and his nephew. There is word of litigation, but litigation involving doctors and their insurers is notoriously slow and it will be difficult to satisfy a court that the Doctor knew that the other kidney was diseased. The defendants may not have to delay for very long for Mr Osman to be deceased, and then there will be no witness as to discussions between the Doctor and himself.'

The ACC(Crime) was known to suffer from the effects of wear and tear on his joints and to hate being kept on his feet for more than a few minutes. Sandy, observing the older man's uneasy transference of his weight from hip to hip, released Honey's hand and got up to offer his chair. Mr Holland subsided onto it gratefully.

'That could certainly explain the Doctor's nervousness,' said Mr Vosp.

'I disagree,' snapped his chief. 'So far we only have evidence of carelessness, possibly amounting to negligence. Removing the wrong organ is a mistake that quite reputable surgeons have made in the past. The Doctor's original words pointed to something criminal.'

'We can guess what he was afraid of,' Honey said. 'It seems that on the day that

Mr Osman's good kidney was removed, a transplant was given to a patient in the Gilberton Clinic.'

'This is all becoming highly irregular if not illegal,' Vosp exclaimed. 'Medical records are supposed to be sacrosanct. There should have been a court order.'

'There will be a court order by tomorrow afternoon,' Mr Holland said grimly. His face, which rarely betrayed any trace of anger, could have been carved out of granite. 'So we are to assume that Mr Osman's good kidney went for transplant, presumably at a price.'

'That is exactly the situation,' Mr Black-house put in. Anyone freshly entering the discussion might well have assumed that he was claiming the credit for the successful investigation.

'Let me see if I have this straight,' said Mr Holland. 'A doctor and a surgeon, under the guise of charitable work, have been matching up donors in famine or disaster areas, desperate for money, with moneyed recipients similarly desperate for organs, and pocketing what in the world of commerce would be called a substantial mark-up. But they have not scrupled to remove a donor's only good kidney. Yes?'

'Yes,' said Honey.

'Leaving aside the legalities for the moment,' Mr Holland said, 'that seems to me to be the most cynically evil deed that I've ever heard of. Given a clear hand, you could prove all this?'

'Given help and facilities and no more obstruction, I think so.'

'Go ahead, then. You'll get the backup.'

'Don't you want to know the name of the recipient of that kidney?' Honey asked.

'I object to this method of questioning,' Vosp said. 'That information is protected. Not even the recipient should know the source of his donor organ. And we are being offered a great deal of hearsay.'

'That wasn't the question,' said Mr Holland. 'I do want to know the identity of the recipient. I want to know it very much.'

'It was a Mr Vosp. Matthew Vosp.'

The silence in the room was unbroken except for a tiny mewing sound as the baby stirred. Then they all began to breathe again in unison.

Mr Holland gave his sweating depute a look blending contempt and reproach. 'And I recall that your brother married into the banking family. He would certainly be able to afford the cost of the operation and an illicit kidney. He was ailing, a year ago, but then made a recovery.'

Vosp's limbs were shaking. Honey had to move her feet aside quickly as he collapsed onto the foot of the bed. 'I knew that my brother had a kidney transplant,' he said. 'I knew nothing about where the kidney came from.'

Detective Superintendent Blackhouse had been listening intently but in silence – waiting, Honey thought, to see which way the argument was going before committing himself. He glared down at Vosp. 'But it was you who gave me firm orders that the Doctor was to be left alone and not investigated. Why would that have been, except that you knew that the Doctor had illicitly obtained a kidney for your brother?'

White-faced, Vosp said, 'Those were Mr Holland's orders.'

'Orders that I permitted you to pass on after considerable persuasion on your part,' the ACC(Crime) said. 'I wondered at the time why you were so impassioned about it, but you harped on the Doctor's reputation for charitable work and you moved heaven and earth to convince me that Dr McGordon was being unjustly harassed. Against my better judgement, I allowed you to persuade me; so I suppose the ultimate responsibility for the very difficult position in which Mr Blackhouse and Inspector Laird have been placed is mine.'

After another moment of fraught silence a babble broke out. Vosp was blustering and Mr Blackhouse was demanding immediate exoneration for himself and, as an afterthought, Honey.

Mr Holland, by seniority added to force of personality, topped them with a firm statement that Vosp was suspended pending a full enquiry. 'And,' he said, 'this is the one place where a doctor could wander freely with a hypodermic syringe. I shall not be easy in my mind until both doctors are confined. We need protection for Inspector Laird, and until it can be organised I want a constable on guard.'

'I know just the man,' Honey said.

Vosp was still protesting but topping all came the voice of young Miss Laird, raised in protest at having been brought into the world against her wishes, then woken by angry voices but left to starve. It was a loud voice and one that nature had designed to be impossible to ignore. There was some attempt to talk above it, but when Sandy handed Honey the baby and Honey began preparations for the feed, there was a hurried exodus. The sound of argument could be heard receding along the corridor.

Sandy was looking fondly at the picture of mother and child but Honey found that motherhood seemed to help the gathering of her wits. 'Go after the Super,' she said. 'Tell him that we've just decided that Allan Dodson is to be another godfather.'

'All right. But why?'

'Can you see him sharing the duty and having to mingle with a mere constable?'

'Clever!'

'I'm not just a pretty face and a set of reproductive organs.' Honey returned her attention to the most beautiful baby in the world, but she was shaking with laughter so that some difficulty was experienced in latching on.

The publishers hope that this book has given you enjoyable reading. Large Print Books are especially designed to be as easy to see and hold as possible. If you wish a complete list of our books please ask at your local library or write directly to:

**Magna Large Print Books**
Magna House, Long Preston,
Skipton, North Yorkshire.
BD23 4ND

This Large Print Book, for people
who cannot read normal print,
is published under the auspices of

## THE ULVERSCROFT FOUNDATION